MW01470174

For Fred,

With best wishes,

Jack

More Shorts in The Dark

By

John A. Curry

authorHOUSE™

1663 LIBERTY DRIVE, SUITE 200
BLOOMINGTON, INDIANA 47403
(800) 839-8640
WWW.AUTHORHOUSE.COM

First published by AuthorHouse 11/03/04

ISBN: 1-4208-0820-6 (sc)

Library of Congress Control Number: 2004098116

Printed in the United States of America
Bloomington, Indiana

This book is printed on acid-free paper.

Also by

JOHN A. CURRY

Loyalty (1999)

Two and Out (2001)

The Irish Corsicans (2002)

Bless Me Father (2003)

Some Shorts in the Dark (2004)

All published by Author House

ACKNOWLEDGMENTS

My thanks to Susan Curry, my daughter-in-law, for her great help with this new collection of short stories.

This anthology is dedicated to all members of my family who have attended the greatest urban university in America: Robert, Susan, and Timothy Curry; Jessica and Nicole Curry; Melissa and Jim Brown; Nancy and Joan Laitinen; Kathy Parrish; Craig MacDonald; Marty Curry.

All hail, Northeastern!

TABLE OF CONTENTS

NOTES

1) "Missing Him Dearly" was written in the winter of 2004, another attempt at a surprise ending.

2) "The Old Girl Friend" was triggered by my high regard for the girl in the picture, a favorite cousin Nancy McPartin.

3) "The Aggrieved" is one of my personal favorites in this collection. Maybe crime does pay.

4) "Lynn, Lynn, the City of Firsts" is my tribute to my home town. The list of firsts will overwhelm you.

5) "The Passenger" – I always come back to crime fiction.

6) "Home Invasion" – Ditto. Both this story and "The Passenger" were written in April, 2004.

7) "Paying Off the Debt" is an excerpt from my first novel <u>Loyalty</u> (1999).

8) "Lynn English vs. Lynn Classical, 1946" – the greatest game ever played between the two rivals and I was there. I love to recapture times gone by.

9) "Trying to Connect" is a selection from my second novel <u>Two and Out</u> (2001).

10) "For Services Rendered" was written while thinking one day that none of us can afford to die.

11) "The Movies of My Youth" helped shape my values and my character. I hope you enjoy these recollections of Hollywood in the 1940's.

12) "The Bus to Foxwoods" was written in the spring of 2004 and is a tribute to seniors everywhere.

13) Every one of my works contains some mention of boxing. In "Sweet as Sugar", I reminisce about one of the all-time greats – Robinson.

14) We all have known "Inspirational People." In this essay I pay tribute to Lynn English's Ruth Hatch, who taught U.S. History so that we learned to think.

15) "The Intervention" allows me to poke a little fun at crisis intervention. I'm only kidding.

16) The anthology concludes with "Jealousy", a crime fiction piece with yet another trick ending.

MISSING HIM DEARLY

She drove his Nissan 240 SX toward Danvers on that road Governor Paul Dever had built back in the 1950's – Route 128, a circumferential highway around Boston that now took longer to navigate than driving into Boston itself. Out the window the sky was a cloudless blue dome, and in the distance the lights of Boston gleamed like diamonds on a necklace.

Was there really such a thing as missing a person, a friend, a lover too much? Her heart told her yes, decidedly yes. She needed to get out more, put an end to her reclusive behavior, meet people, participate in life, come alive again.

So she had placed the personal ad and made the date – her first ever blind date.

But as she roared up the hill opposite the North Shore Shopping Mall, she thought again of Matt. She wiped a small tear from her eye, cursing herself for potentially spoiling her mascara. She slowed a bit and lowered the rearview mirror to observe the damage she had done.

Not bad, she thought, studying her image in the mirror. Not bad for a woman close to fifty years old now. Her auburn hair, usually pulled tight to her skull, was full to her shoulders, avoiding that look of sharp severity that came with an unflattering bun. She wore just a touch of translucent lip gloss and no other make-up or jewelry. After all, she did not want to appear too forward or too anxious, too assertive.

She glanced down at her black business suit, hemmed at a conservative knee length. She wore sturdy black shoes with low heels to lessen the impact of what she believed were otherwise shapely legs. She would appear businesslike and friendly, but not too nervous or sad.

Kay Simpson turned onto Route 62 in Danvers, heading east to the Danversport Yacht Club, now about a mile up on her right. And found herself thinking once again about Matt. Why couldn't she put that part of her life behind her? Although she constantly strived to do so, Matt was always right there on the cusp.

They had been married at St. Joseph's Church in Lynn on a late summer day just like this one. She remembered the boyish hank of black hair that had fallen toward his brow and that impish glint that animated his dark green eyes in his youth. He had been such a handsome man, such a dedicated, loving mate, doting on her, buying her expensive gifts, worshiping her.

And in turn, she had come to love her childhood sweetheart. They had attended St. Joseph's Institute together from grade one to grade eight, "just friends" as he had put it in those days. But in high school, at Lynn English, friendship had turned to love and, as Frank Sinatra had so aptly phrased it, love and marriage came together like a horse and carriage.

What made this new involvement especially difficult were the ever-present memories of Matt. As she parked in the vast expanse of the Yacht Club lot, she thought of how proud she had been when Matt had attained tenure at Northeastern University. Her Matt a respected scholar, an expert in nineteenth century prose, a star in the University's firmament, beloved and respected by his colleagues and students.

She had enjoyed the many faculty socials and the opportunity to socialize with the intelligencia, to demonstrate that Professor Simpson had a wife who could mix and talk on a wide variety of topics, even though she had never actually worked after finishing her B.S. degree. She had wanted children first and foremost, and had stayed home to raise Ray, Sheila, and Gail. Now all three lived so far distant —- in Chicago, Santa Fe, and Sarasota. She was now basically alone. As the song says, "with only the memories".

When Matt had become sick with the cancer, she had never strayed from his side. Initially, he had been devastated by the news that he had contacted prostate cancer, but her self-assurance, her optimism, her tender care had all contributed to his recovery. That had occurred more than four years ago now. And with the help of good support programs, he had regained his sexual prowess —- until just recently.

God, how she had loved him, she thought, as she walked toward the entrance to the restaurant. At the thought of Matt and of her loss, she once again felt a small tear forming. Stop it! Stop dwelling on him!

she chastised herself. Move on! Starting tonight – move on to a new life, to a new beginning. Form new relationships. Become alive once again.

She walked toward the circular bar and found a seat facing the entrance. She studied her watch — 5:45 p.m. She always preferred to arrive early for any scheduled appointment, and, particularly tonight, meeting him for the first time, she wanted the advantage of being settled and comfortable and prepared.

"What'll it be?" a short broad-shouldered young man asked her. In the background piped-in music told of how somebody had done someone wrong.

"A Cape Codder," she replied evenly.

Anxiously, she turned toward the entrance and quickly stopped tearing at the paper napkin in her hands. Calm down, girl! You've met men before. Stop acting like such a fool.

Most people gathered near the entrance at the maitre d' station were in couples or in groups. Virtually no one was alone, but he would be, and he should appear now almost any minute.

She drank some of the Cape Codder and reached for the cheese and crackers. The Yacht Club was one of the few places left in Massachusetts that gave you something to eat with a drink.

And there he was, standing there for a brief moment in the archway, looking her way. He appeared tall and urbane, in his middle forties. He wore an impeccably tailored light gray suit that flattered an athletic frame.

As he approached the bar, she focused on the color of his skin, a smooth olive-brown complexion reflecting a life spent in the sun.

"Kay Simpson?" he inquired, his handshake docile, his demeanor calm and controlled as he slid onto the seat next to her. "I'm Robert Cochrane."

"Yes, I'm pleased to meet you, Mr. Cochrane," she replied.

"Please. Call me Robert," he said, his teeth gleaming. "And may I call you Kay?"

"Yes."

Robert not Bob, she noted.

She relaxed a bit, dealing with a gentleman was such a relief. For days now she had wondered about placing the personal ad. Who would appear – Dr. Jekyll or Mr. Hyde?

"Yes, sir, what'll you have?" the bartender asked.

"Would you prefer to go right in to eat?" Robert asked.

"I'm in no hurry," she replied. "Let's just sit and enjoy a drink first."

As he ordered, she considered her last comment. This was all so new to her. Stop being so damn assertive, she cautioned herself.

"So tell me about yourself," Robert said, smiling over his glass, his words almost staged. Another guy in love with himself. Nothing like Matt at all. Matt – so tender, loving, so willing to please. Matt was – stop thinking about Matt. Concentrate on the present, not the past!

"What do you need to know?"

"Well, for starters, and maybe for an ice breaker, what made you place the ad in the personals?"

How much should she tell him, particularly on first meeting?

"I was filtering through some magazines at the mall and before I knew it I decided to write."

Robert gave her the stagy smile once again. "I'm glad you did. It's a big step. I know it's not easy for a woman…"

She suppressed her defensiveness. "I did think about it for a long time before I got up the courage to write. Do you get many responses to the ad?" she asked, trying to steer the conversation away from herself.

He locked in on her before smiling broadly. "I'd rather not say."

"I understand."

"Could I say something without offending you?"

"Go ahead."

"Are you sure you're comfortable with this? I mean you seem…"

She signaled for the barman. "We're ready for the bill."

She felt the crimson tide running through her face. Why couldn't she just relax? Let things happen. Stop being such a tight-ass, such a dominating presence.

Looking across at the huge mirror, she saw that Robert was still smiling. Maybe she wasn't being received as poorly as her own perception.

"Let's go have some dinner," she said, placing her hand lightly on top of his.

"Sure," he said, rising.

He took command before she could, signaling to the maitre d', raising two fingers on high. Out the huge plate glass window, small vessels approached their moorings, their weekend commanders ready now for drinks and dinner. Small children scurried from good-sized motor launches and sailboats, while old guys who looked like Michael Douglas escorted shapely twenty-year-olds along the wharf.

The waiter was on them as soon as they sat, and for that she was grateful. She needed to gather her thoughts while Robert ordered for them, then say what she wanted to say confidently, try to make a good impression.

"I wasn't completely honest back there," she finally said. "This isn't easy for me. My husband Matt's only been gone…"

"You don't need to explain, Kay," he interrupted, placing his hand on hers. "I don't need to hear about the past. In fact, I prefer we not get into it."

She tensed once again. "All right then. Let's just talk about the here and now. Did you receive the letter?"

While the waiter placed their food in front of them, no one spoke.

"Will there be anything else, sir?" he asked.

"We're fine," Robert replied.

"You're absolutely sure you want to proceed?" he asked her.

"I'm positive."

"Do you have the second half of the payment with you?"

She opened her Coach pocketbook, searched out the envelope, and slid it across to him.

"So he's at the address you gave me on the phone?"

"Yes," she said evenly, the tension easing out of her now, her determination driving her forward. "He's living with the bimbo, the student he's been screwing for the last year, the one he left me for."

Robert didn't appear very much interested in her feelings. He finished the last of his filet mignon and savored the last drops of a 1990 Altesino Brunello di Montalcino, just arrived in their cellar according to the waiter.

"So when will it happen?" she asked.

"You don't need to know that," he replied.

"But it will look like an accident?"

"Absolutely."

She sat back, the wine getting to her, bringing on a wave of satisfaction.

"Good," she said.

She thought again of Matt. She would miss him dearly. He had been a good friend, an extraordinary lover, a reasonably good husband, until he began thinking with his pecker instead of his brain. Too bad. But with his insurance money she would travel, meet new lovers. Maybe someone who could be faithful.

"Anything else?" she asked Robert.

"No. We'll never contact one another again."

She stood and extended a hand. "It's been a pleasure doing business with you, Robert."

THE OLD GIRLFRIEND

For part of the month he'd known her, it had been difficult for Barry to get an accurate idea of just how spectacular her body might be. She always wore baggy clothes that did nothing to flatter the physique she was revealing to him now. She had a belly as taut as a trampoline with not a sag in evidence anywhere.

She approached the bed and dropped her bra and panties on the floor. Sitting on the edge of the bed for a brief moment, she gazed at him. "Are you up for another?"

He was always up for another. And another. Viagra allowed him to perform for long periods, reinforcing his belief that Barry Considine still possessed the goods to keep the young fillies interested.

Later when they just lay there contemplating one another's navels, she brought up the ring issue again, much to his dismay.

"How long have we been together now, Pumpkin?"

Pumpkin, ugh. As if she didn't know the length of their involvement right to the hour and minute. "A month, give or take a day, my dear. A month I'll never forget. Every day with you has been unforgettable," he said, stroking her ear. At least the sex was, he thought.

"Flatterer," she said in that pouty Marilyn Monroe voice.

"I mean it," he replied.

"Pumpkin, then why can't we go to Tiffany's up at Copley Place and get that ring I was telling you about?"

Lately, she had also been talking about moving in. God, there was no such thing as privacy anymore.

Rita was leaning into him when she spotted the photograph where he had placed it on the mantel late last night. She stared at it for a moment and then swung her long legs to the floor so she could look at it.

"She's attractive," she finally said, ungraciously.

"That's my old girlfriend. Yes, she is, isn't she?" Barry replied smugly.

Barry turned and stared at the picture of him on the flat sands of Lynn Beach, standing beside the smiling tall blonde.

Rita tried to blink back her curiosity. "Who took the picture?" she asked.

"My friend Paul."

"I love her smile. Who is she?"

"Just an old girl friend."

"She has such a beautiful smile."

Barry looked at the photo across the room. "But that was her problem. She smiled at everyone."

Rita, the ultimate feminist, came to the defense of the unknown woman. "What's that supposed to mean?"

Barry sat at the edge of the bed and searched out his shorts.

"Maybe I just didn't like the way she smiled," he finally said. "Everywhere we went together she'd be beaming that shitty smile at some guy. Didn't matter if they were young or decrepit, in shape or four hundred pounds, she'd grin that dumb smile at them."

"God! Maybe she was just being friendly!" Rita exclaimed.

"She was too happy. Always giggling, smiling, laughing. Like a damn hyena. I'd catch her looking out the window smiling at the moon, the sun, the rain. If it was raining shit, she'd be smiling."

Rita started to feel a slight chill.

"In fact when we lived together she'd come down to breakfast, all happy like she'd hit the lottery, looking perfect, not a hair out of place, the smile on her face… looking like a god damn monkey," he said.

"Well, what did you want? Some sad sack sharing a bed with you?"

"I wanted a different expression. Some emotion other than a leering, happy puss. I wanted her to have a different approach, a different look just for me. After all, wasn't I special? Wasn't I the one she supposedly loved? You know what I mean?"

Rita moved across the room, picked up the photo, and studied it. "No, I don't," she finally said.

"No, I don't suppose you do," he replied tersely.

"I'm really surprised at you, Barry. What are you some kind of control freak?"

"Me?" he pointed to himself, an innocent look crossing his face. "No. In fact, I just got rid of her."

"You dumped her?"

"In a way."

"Because you didn't like her smiling all the time?"

"Precisely." He paused for a beat. "Well, I didn't really dump her, but I did put a stop to that happy bullshit."

Rita stared at the smirk on his handsome face and then walked to the closet and found her clothes. She began dressing. "Could I ask how you stopped her from being so happy, from smiling? I mean, I just don't get it."

"I have a friend who shall remain anonymous. He'd never met her so for my providing a particular sum he... Let's just say the whole thing went well. No complications. And now I don't have her staring at me and everyone else with love light in her eyes anymore."

"You're shittin' me."

Barry stood to stroke her face. "I love you, Rita. If we're going to be together..."

"I don't believe this. I don't believe you. This can't be happening," Rita said, shrinking from his touch.

"You had that girl killed because you didn't have all her attention, her complete attention?"

"I'm not admitting to anything, but love must be all encompassing, Rita. My love must be completely devoted to me."

"You must be a monster! I never saw this side of you, Barry. I…I just don't know what to say."

She started toward the door.

"But I love you, Rita. We'll go out today, pick out the ring. You can move in with me. We could…"

She bolted from the room, barely remembering her handbag.

Barry followed her to the foyer and locked the door behind her. Turning to the bar, he poured himself a double scotch, walked to the window and stared at the billowing, angry waves crashing against the seawall across the street from his Lynn Beach condominium.

Why were women so possessive? he mused. Why couldn't they be more like men? Always talking about love, about moving in, about fancy rings, and travel to exotic locations. Always after the man and his wallet.

He walked toward the bedroom and picked up the photo. The picture of his cousin Nancy from Quincy always proved invaluable whenever the predators started circling his wagon.

THE AGGRIEVED

"I want a divorce."

Is that what she said, right out of the blue, as if she wanted a glass of water, so calmly, so controlled, so unfeeling, not even measuring its devastating effect on me?

"You what?"

"I want a divorce."

We were standing in the kitchen of our home in Nordeast, as locals sometimes called it, in Minneapolis, in an old Eastern European part of town which had grown much more integrated through the years. It was now an upper middle-class neighborhood of older homes with big screened porches and flat full lawns, with trains rumbling off toward Minneapolis sounding in the far distance.

"What's wrong?" I finally stammered.

"Oh, Sam, I don't have to tell you how things have been going, do I really?"

Ingrid stood there at the refrigerator door, palming the small cubes of ice into her glass of straight whisky, her back turned to me, her dark, ravenous hair worn today in a ponytail, her side profile delineating a pale olive complexion.

"I don't understand," I replied, groping to regain some measure of composure.

Ingrid turned toward me, those Nordic ice blue eyes locked on me, her confidence, as always, right there to be seen.

"It's another man, isn't it?" I asked hesitantly, my decorum now practically spent.

"Let's sit and discuss this intelligently," she replied, sipping on the whisky as she moved toward me. "Do you want something to drink?"

"A Coke."

"See. There's a perfect example of our growing incompatibility. You see me having a hard drink, and you want a Coke."

"It's another man, isn't it?" I persisted.

She placed her drink on the kitchen table and walked back to the refrigerator and found the Coke. She poured it into a glass, skipping the ice. She knew I'd rather fill the whole glass with the Coke instead of depositing a glacial layer of ice over your one inch of drink like they do in most restaurants.

"Here," the iceberg said, handing it to me. "How long have we been married now, Sam?" She asked as if she didn't know the answer, setting me up, getting ready to lower the boom on me coldly and cruelly.

"What the hell's that got to do with this?" I asked disconsolately.

"Six years, Sam. Six years since we tied the knot, and now you're sinking me like an anchor."

"That's a fine thing to say," I replied forlornly.

"I don't want to cause you any undue pain, Sam."

"Yes, you fuckin' do."

She placed a warm hand on top of mine. "We were too young, Sam. A couple of young teachers who thought they would be forever in love…"

"I loved you then, and I love you now," I said, trying hard to stifle a sob.

Ingrid threw back some of the whisky. "Sam, I was a twenty-five-year-old, first year faculty member at the university."

"So what? So now you're a thirty-one-year-old tenured faculty member."

She stared at me with those eyes to die for. "I've changed. You've changed."

"Bullshit."

She breathed an audible sigh. "Take our sex life."

"What about it?"

"You need Viagra to have sex?"

"You weren't complaining last night."

"Just because I didn't say anything last night doesn't mean I'm not complaining, Sam. A guy your age – thirty-two – needs to take Viagra to have a boner?"

"I take it to sustain the performance, to make it more pleasureable for you and for me," I said defensively.

"You watch too much TV," she said.

"What's that supposed to mean?"

"It means just because some asshole is throwing a football through tires while the voiceover talks about the Levitra putting the guy "in the zone", not every woman wants to face all-night boners with a smiling face."

"Oh, yeah?"

"Yeah. You notice the woman says nothing. She's just the object."

"Well, it helps me."

"That's what I mean. At thirty-two you need help?"

"My doctor says it's a temporary thing."

"Yeah? Well, he doesn't have to live with you."

"So this is about sex?" I asked.

"Not just sex. The sex problem is indicative of other problems between us."

"Like what?"

"Like you don't have any fun. I'm loose, liberal, looking to have a good time. You're uptight, always working. Then there's the sports."

"The sports?"

"Yeah, you might as well live with those ESPN guys. You know, Chris what's-his-face and those other clowns thinking they're real funny men tossing out rhymes like they're Walt Whitman – 'Randy Moss caught the toss', 'Kevin from Heaven Garnett', she mimicked. "Every night the asshole's yelling, 'He could go all the way!'"

"You used to like sports," I said.

"Right. But not twenty-four seven. It's just another example of our going in different directions."

"It's a guy, isn't it?"

"What are you, a broken record?"

"At least be honest with me."

Ingrid stood, poured herself some more of the Jack, and sat back down. "I didn't go looking for another man, Sam. I want you to understand. It followed from these other problems we've been talking about."

I focused on her. "Who is he?"

"You know him," she said evenly. "It's Arthur."

"Arthur Strong?" I replied incredulously.

"Yes. Arthur Strong."

"I can't believe it."

"Believe it."

"But he's our colleague, our friend..." I said, finding it all so hard to digest. One body blow after another.

Ingrid ran a finger around the rim of her glass. "I don't want to cause you pain, Sam, but..."

"You said that already."

She turned on her sincere look, the staged one that pled for understanding. Understanding for her position, but no one else's.

"Arthur's being a friend was just what I needed, Sam. With you and I drifting apart the last year."

I raised a hand in protest. "I never felt we were drifting."

"Well, if you had gotten your head out of your books, paid a little more attention…"

"So how long's this been going on?"

Ingrid looked to her fingers for wisdom. "About ten months ago, after classes, I was having a drink over at the U of M pub on Churchill? Arthur walked in when I was particularly vulnerable – I mean in need of a friend."

"I never did like that sanctimonious son of a bitch. Any asshole who digs around in rock formations…"

"It's called geology, Sam."

"He's a second rater. Here you're married to a world class criminologist…"

"With little time for me."

"He's a pansy for God's sake," I snickered.

John A. Curry

She paused for a long beat before responding. "I'm not going to get into a name calling contest with you, Sam. I just want us to go our separate ways, split all property 50-50. We have no children. We should be able to part amicably."

I studied the Coke glass, trying to anchor myself. When you don't see it coming, the words are doubly hurtful, shutting off your ability to think clearly, taking you downward into a vortex of numbness and melancholy.

When I looked at her again, she was tossing me that look that six years ago I had caught in my hip pocket. That sweet, demure, sexy stare that attracted you right away, reminding me of her near look-alike, the high cheekboned Ali McGraw in "Love Story," a preppy, confident, together girl. I had been sitting in the library at the University of Minnesota researching the Oklahoma City bombing case when she had sat across from me. For a few minutes I studied my brief but in quick time I felt her observing me with that stare. "Hi" she said, as I looked up.

"Hi, yourself," I said, sitting up a bit straighter.

"Are you a student?," she whispered, leaning forward.

"I'm Sam Ellison, I'm a first year professor. In Criminal Justice," I added quickly.

"Here? You are? Me, too. I just started teaching in the English Department this fall," she had said.

That's how it had begun, and now she was saying something, her words knifing through my fog of pain, saying something about moving out next week. I wasn't really absorbing much of it. I just wanted to go some place and hide.

—

What exactly was it that made me decide to kill her? The look? That uncaring, heartless look those last few days before she moved out? The arrogance? That condescending manner whenever she did bring up the subject again during that last week? "You'll be all right, Sam. You enjoy your own company. You'll have your work." Like Bogart telling Bergman, "We'll always have Paris." Yeah, except Paul Henreid got the girl.

The rejection? Yes, above all else, it was the rejection that decided matters for me. She had dumped me like a sack of potatoes, unconcerned about my needs and the love still burning like a cancer within me. She had trampled on my self-esteem, the leading criminologist in America dropped for Arthur Strong, an absolute nothing.

Stupid Arthur Strong. Everything about the dullard reeked of tentativeness. Three weeks after Ingrid left me, I sat at the elongated bar in the University of Minnesota pub, watching him in the mirror.

He sensed me staring at him as he sat alone eating some kind of dreadful meatloaf. If he took a doggie bag home, the dog would refuse it. He sat there pasty-faced, short, a geologist without portfolio, a popinjay of no consequence or distinction. What could she possibly see in him?

After a time he nodded to me and I nodded back. Maybe by feigning pleasantries I could find out something about Ingrid. I stood and walked to his table.

"Hello, Arthur," I said, standing there.

"Glad to see you, Sam," he said in an unsure voice as he reached awkwardly for a roll, a faint bead of perspiration appearing on his forehead. "I saw you on television last night," he says. "The St. Paul Strangler case?"

"Yes, I hope my contributions were helpful to the police," I replied modestly.

My standing there was obviously causing him pain. I sensed he didn't know what to do with me so I sat in order to make him more uncomfortable.

"Your profile was brilliant," he said.

Looking at the fool, the unscholarly, weak fool, was what made me think of another possible approach to ending Ingrid's life.

"How's Ingrid?" I asked.

"Fine, Sam. She's fine," he replied, almost tipping over a glass of water.

"Please let her know I was asking for her," I said, forcing my lips to smile.

"I will," he said, avoiding my eyes.

I stood to leave but then sat down abruptly. "You know, Arthur, these things happen in the course of life.

37

Granted it hurts, but I want you to know I've moved on. I'm gradually getting over her," I lied. "I just want you to know there are no hard feelings."

For the first time he looked me squarely in the eye. "I'm so pleased you're not upset with me, Sam."

"Why be uncivil?" I replied evenly. "And how is your work going, Arthur?"

A frown creased his face. "I've just finished my first book and am readying it for publication, and, hopefully, for tenure."

"And what does it concern?" I asked, feigning interest in what I was sure was some dull discourse on rock formations in Afghanistan or some other dreadful place, another contribution to true scholarly research that would sit on library shelves with no one paying particular interest for decades to come.

"It's my treatise regarding the formation of rocks in Arizona near Monument Valley," he replied, confirming my evaluation. Arizona, Afghanistan, what was the difference? I had learned all I needed to know about Monument Valley through John Ford's westerns.

"It sounds fascinating," I said, pausing then for a beat. "Arthur, are you open to a suggestion?" I asked.

"By all means."

"You may know my publisher is Doubleday. They do all sorts of things. With your permission I would be pleased to pass them some excerpts from your work and see if they would be interested."

Arthur beamed his coast-to-coast smile, accentuating the pock marks on his white face. "You'd do that for me?"

"I think I could at least get someone to look it over for you," I replied cheerfully.

—

I saw Arthur again perhaps a month later. My publisher had reacted to his moronic treatise as I knew they would. They had no particular interest in his lackluster writing or his mundane hypotheses. They did, however, suggest a small Midwestern publisher to me after I pressed them for some sort of positive response.

I kept Arthur waiting for another week before I decided to lunch at the faculty club one bright spring afternoon, knowing that he would be there nibbling as usual on some dreadful lunch.

"Arthur, what a surprise!" I said, approaching his table. "I was going to call you this afternoon."

"Sam! Nice to see you! Won't you join me for lunch?"

I hesitated for a beat. "Well, of course," I finally said. "It's better than eating alone."

As I slid into the seat opposite him, I could sense his apprehension and his desire to learn of my effort on his behalf. I didn't prolong the agony. Smiling effusively, I dressed up the evaluation. "I've got some good news, Arthur. Doubleday has some interest, but is leaning heavily toward fiction this year, based on the success of their <u>DaVinci Code</u>. However, they have strong connections with Neimus over in Davenport, Iowa, and after review, Neimus has agreed to publish your work."

Arthur's lack of confidence was replaced by a spreading smile. "Honest to God?" he finally replied, some of his soup leaking now from the corner of his mouth. Honest to God indeed. What did Ingrid see in this nitwit?

"I don't know how to thank you, Sam. I've had such trouble with this book and now – and now I'll have a good chance at tenure. Thanks to you."

If I had my way, Mr. Arthur Popinjay Strong (now wasn't that surname a clear misnomer, I thought) would be going to jail, not to tenure.

I waved my hand dismissively. "Think nothing of it, Arthur. I'm only too pleased to help."

After I had ordered, I asked my question. "And how is Ingrid these days, Arthur?"

My new-found best buddy paused before answering. "Sam, could I ask you a question in the strictest confidence?"

"Of course, Arthur."

"What caused you and Ingrid to divorce? I mean I know her version…"

I drank some of my tea before responding. "Why do you ask, Arthur? Is she complaining about you?"

I thought he might fall off the chair.

"Why yes," he said. "But why do you ask?"

"Well, like you, I consider myself a scientist, a researcher. Now by my estimates you and Ingrid have been seeing each other for about a year now. That's just about when she started complaining about me."

Arthur's eyes widened, taking on the look of large buttons.

"To answer your question, I would say sex was the primary reason for our break-up," I said.

He lowered his head, staring into his glass of wine.

"Is that the problem?" I said, softening my voice, a friend in need.

He looked up quickly. "I really don't feel like talking about it," he said, his voice quivering.

"Of course not," I agreed.

"What was there about your sex life that bothered her?" he suddenly blurted out.

I ran my index finger around the rim of the cup. "My insatiable appetite for sex, for one thing," I lied. "But my prowess still wasn't enough for her."

"What do you mean?" he asked, frowning.

"I found out she was seeing other people."

"You mean me?"

I shook my head. "You, of course, Arthur. But there were others long before you."

He looked like I had hit him in the ass with a shovel. "I don't understand, Sam."

"She was always going out, talking for extended periods on the phone on what she claimed was faculty business, coming home with expensive presents that she claimed she bought for herself," I said. "After a time, I suddenly realized I was not paranoid. Eventually she told me about you, and that's when I asked her for the divorce."

"You asked her for the divorce?" Arthur asked, practically vaulting from his seat.

"Why, yes," I replied calmly.

"But Ingrid told me she asked you for the divorce because…"

"Go ahead," I nodded encouragingly.

"Because you didn't pay enough attention to her, you didn't…"

"Let me guess, Arthur. I didn't provide enough sex, right."

"Yes. Among other things."

Having planted the seed, I let him down easily. "When two people divorce, Arthur, they each have their own version of the same set of facts. It's like Rashomon, each party has his or her own idea of the truth. But why are we talking about this?" I added.

"I love her, you know," the fool said in that whispering voice.

"But of course you do," I replied.

"I don't know what I'd do if she left me," he said, placing a quivering hand to his forehead.

"Probably survive as I have," I said, trying for a touch of humor.

"I shouldn't be telling you this, Sam, but I worship her."

"And I assume she you," I replied supportively. "Perhaps she's changed."

"I'm not as strong as you, Sam. If she were ever to leave me…" His voice tailed off.

I swallowed the last of the Earl Gray. "Well, there's probably a good chance she's reformed with your help. I'm afraid I wasn't the right man to contain her interest in others."

"She complains about me as a sexual partner," he confided. "And she complains about the time I don't spend with her."

"You open to advice?" I asked.

"Of course."

"Don't become paranoid, my boy. That's what hurt me with her. But use your scientific intellect. Observe her. Chart out her time, who she spends it with, and I'm sure, in time, you'll conclude she's faithful to you."

"That's good advice," the toad said.

"After all, you have no hard evidence of any infidelity, do you?"

"No."

"Be the scientist you are, Arthur." A zero, I almost added.

———

The Chinese say that nature, time, and patience are the three great physicians. Maybe so, but they also can serve other purposes, particularly mine.

I didn't see Arthur again until a month had passed, when I made it my business to visit his office one Tuesday afternoon when I knew he would be conducting hours. He sat behind a wooden desk in one corner of a barren room with similar desks in each quadrant, the room befitting the academic stature of the rock pounder.

"Good afternoon, Arthur," I said, advancing to the straight back chair aside his desk. We were the only two in the room.

"Why, Sam! What brings you by?"

"I just delivered a set of grades to the registrar so I thought I'd see how you're doing."

"Please sit down."

"And what's happening with your book?" I asked.

"It's coming along," he answered forlornly, as if the book was not paramount in his mind. "Thanks to you," he added.

"When will it be published?"

"They've asked me to make some changes, but sometime in the next two months I believe."

"Wonderful."

He cast me a glance that said otherwise.

"Is something wrong, Arthur?" I asked gently . The popinjay was always in a state of manic depression. A mental defective if ever I met one.

"It's Ingrid," he replied, raising a shaky hand to his chin. "I'm completely frustrated by her behavior. I'm drinking too much, Sam, and I'm constantly upset."

"What's the problem?" I asked sympathetically.

"Do you remember our last conversation?"

"Of course."

"Well, I followed your advice. I've been observing her patterns which are in complete contrast to her words."

I raised a quizzical brow. "I'm not following you, Arthur."

He emitted a huge sigh. "She says she loves me, she swears her fidelity, but there are these other signs…"

"Tell me about them."

He glanced quickly about the room, as if he expected her to appear at any moment. "You must think me paranoid."

"Heavens, no, Arthur. Remember I lived with her, too."

He nodded furtively. "She says I'm obsessed, keeping her practically a prisoner of war."

"Funny that. She said the same thing to me."

"She comes home late, claiming she works at the office."

"Yes. That's possible."

"But on two occasions, when she claimed she was working there on a research project, I called and no one answered."

"She could have been elsewhere in the building," I suggested helpfully.

"And then once or twice I've seen her talking to her colleague from the English Department, talking for extended periods, touching hands…"

"Where was this?"

"At English Department socials to which I was also invited."

"Touching, you said?"

"I'm afraid so," he said, his voice quivering. "Looking like intimates."

"That certainly seems suspicious," my helpful self replied.

"I'm beside myself with worry," he said. "I wish I had your strength, Sam. Walking away from her the way you did. I am obsessed with her. I know I am."

"I hesitate to add to your concern," I said just at the right time.

Arthur arched his brow in confusion. "What do you mean?"

"I shouldn't really…"

"Please, Sam, tell me."

"It's probably nothing, Arthur."

"Let me be the judge of that," he insisted.

"Well, yesterday – Monday – I was over at the Mall of America doing my shopping. I just needed some new boots, and …"

"Sam, could you come to the point," the toad said.

"Of course. I'm sorry. I saw Ingrid holding hands with this handsome young man. She didn't see me, but…"

"Holding hands?" he gasped.

"Well, he also had his arm around her waist," I lied. "He then kissed her."

He seemed to crumple within himself. For a few seconds he studied the papers on his desk. "Would you mind leaving me along, Sam," he finally said. "I hope you understand. I don't know what I'm going to do."

I stood to go. "Nothing drastic now Arthur. She's not worth it," I said, planting my final seed.

—

I was sitting in my publisher's office outlining my next project, when I received the news.

"So Robert, I'm planning a book based on the child abduction case down in Sarasota," I was saying as a light rain drummed against a huge plate glass overlooking Fifth Avenue.

"What will be the angle?"

"How loose the courts are in letting filth like Joseph Smith out on the streets. Look, the guy had thirteen convictions and, most recently, violated his parole twice and yet the judge down there was asleep at the switch. He never called him in despite notifications from the parole officer."

"I like it," Robert Fuller, my editor, replied.

There was a light knock on his door followed by the appearance of a pert, lanky brunette. "I'm sorry to interrupt, but there's a call from Minneapolis for you, Professor Ellison. A Captain Moroney from the MPD."

"Really?" I tinted my fingers below my chin. "You can put it through," I directed.

"I'll put it on the speaker if you wish," Robert said.

"Please do."

A raspy voice immediately permeated the room. "Professor Ellison?"

"Hello, Captain. Nice to hear your voice once again," I said.

"I'm afraid I have some bad news for you," Moroney said, the voice straining now. He paused for a moment. "Your ex-wife has been found bludgeoned to death."

I gasped audibly. "My God, Captain, what happened?"

"You do know her live-in – I mean her companion – Professor Arthur Strong, I believe, Professor? He appears to have attacked her in her sleep with a hammer, and then took his own life with a pistol."

I emitted another gasp, louder this time. "My God!"

"He left a note, Professor. It's definitely a murder-suicide," Moroney said.

"What did he say in the note?"

"I'll read it to you. 'Love is not enough. Trust is the real key to a good relationship, and once it is broken it is difficult to rebuild. May God forgive me.' "

I didn't reply right away.

"Professor? Are you still there?"

"I'm sorry, Captain. I was just wondering what led him to that conclusion."

LYNN, LYNN, THE CITY OF FIRSTS

It is most certainly a fact that at age seventy we tend to reflect too much, to dwell on things past, frequently with the hope of correcting them, or on the future, with the hope of outliving it. To a grievous fault I love to think on the city of my birth, of my coming of age, and of its importance in both my personal and professional development.

You have all heard the dumb ditty about "Lynn, Lynn, the City of Sin, you never come out the way you came in." Right? Let's start by correcting that fallacious baloney.

Try instead, "Lynn, Lynn, the City of Firsts." How's this for an impressive list: America's first jet engine was built at General Electric in Lynn in 1942; the first professional night baseball game in America was played in Lynn in 1927; Julia Callahan, the founder of the Parent-Teacher Association movement, was a Lynner; the first woman elected to the American Academy of Arts and Sciences, Maria Mitchell, was from Lynn; the first tannery in our country was built in Lynn in 1632; the first air mail drop occurred in Lynn in 1912; the first electric trolley in Massachusetts ran from Lynn in 1888; the first school of dance established in America was started in Lynn in 1672; the Constitution, the first ship in the U.S. Navy, was built by Edmund Hart of Lynn; Lydia Pinkham, the first woman in advertising, hailed from Lynn; and the first crowd of 20,000 plus at a high school football game in New England occurred in Lynn in 1946.

Do you know of another city that can match that list?

In 1940, when I was six years old, my city offered its young the best of two worlds. Located just ten miles north of Boston, Lynn's long, winding coastline featured endless stretches of sandy beach with the Atlantic hovering in the distance, allowing us a virtual paradise of enjoyment and exploration. In sharp contrast stood a vibrant downtown of huge department stores, small family-owned businesses of every type, nine movie theatres, three five-and-ten cent stores, automats, restaurants of all sizes – a downtown frequented by over 100,000 residents, many of them employed at the G.E. as the country readied for World War II.

In my youth, my friends and I never did learn how to pit school, church, parents, and neighborhood against one another to our advantage. On the contrary, the greatest single contributor to our forming a value system was exactly the way we interacted with those institutions. They were one and together in teaching us right from wrong. Go home and tell your mother or father the nun at St. Joseph's Institute had upbraided you and be ready to have the parent do the same. Miss church one Sunday and be assured the school would be ringing your home to inform your parents of your indiscretion. Say something out of line to a neighbor, and be ready to visit your parent's wrath. Somewhere along the line, beginning with the Baby Boomers in the 60's, we lost those tight connections, especially when parents decided to become "friends" with their offspring, rather than guardians, but that's another story.

The City of Firsts presented countless joys to a young boy of six. I remember walking alone on Union Street (no fear of perverts then) and marveling at the sights and sounds along one of Lynn's main thoroughfares.

At the top of the street stood McAuliffe's Pharmacy with its round stools and rich delights such as ten-cent vanilla frappes. A few stores south was Frank Yee's Laundry, where I brought my dad's shirts to the friendly, boisterous yammerings of its immigrant owner. Just a bit further along Trask's Bakery beckoned me toward a window replete with Danish pastries and custard pies.

A hundred yards south brought me virtually every Saturday or Sunday to the majestic Paramount Theater, a palace unto itself. A small box office opened to an opulent inclined lobby, perhaps thirty yards long and thirty yards wide. One could follow it to a winding staircase on both the left and right, each of which led to a vast balcony. Or you could continue on the incline toward five bronze plated doors opening to five distinct aisles and the massive orchestra itself.

In 1940 all children twelve and under were sheparded into the first few rows of aisle number one, the better to control our behavior, no one particularly concerned that we could all end up cross-eyed. But that didn't matter to me, not when I could sit alone in the dark and fantasize as celluloid images played across the screen, images from the dream factories of MGM, Twentieth Century Fox, and Paramount.

It was there that I saw Judy Garland come of age in "For Me and My Gal" (1942), witnessed Gary Cooper, in glorious Technicolor, fighting off Canadian revolutionists and scary Indians in Cecil B. DeMille's "Northwest Mounted Police" (1940). It's where I got into serious trouble with my mother that same year by watching Alice Faye and Betty Grable doing their "Sheik of Araby" number from "Tin Pan Alley" (1940), which when coupled with the latest Charlie Chan "B" feature, a newsreel, a cartoon, and previews of coming attractions – all seen twice – took more than six hours.

I can remember standing in line in 1940 to see "Gone with the Wind" (1939). Kind of heavy stuff for a six-year-old? Not at all. Through a carefully controlled production code at the time, all movies were deemed acceptable for the young. In the movies of the 40's, good always triumphed, evil was always vanquished, and the good guys wore white hats. There was no sex and no swearing.

The Paramount was the crown jewel of Lynn's movie palaces, but my favorite was down Union Street about another hundred yards. There the Warner Brothers had sandwiched a theater among three five-and-ten cent stores – Woolworth's, McClellan's, and Kresge's. I would first visit one of them to obtain my nickel jelly beans or marshmallow peanuts, rather than pay the theater's outrageous prices. Then I would enter the Warner which featured a stable of my favorite stars thematically united in gritty, urban social dramas – Cagney, Bogart, Bette Davis, John Garfield, Edward G. Robinson, to name just a few.

At the end of Union Street, in Central Square itself, the Capitol Theater offered twin bills from Columbia or Universal Studios, coupled with a live vaudeville show and a Three Stooges comedy. Talk about a bang for the buck – I mean for eleven cents.

If you missed the first-run double features at the three principal theaters (movies no matter how popular played one week only from Wednesday through Tuesday), then you simply caught them at the Olympia next to Anthony Athanas' original Hawthorne

Restaurant, or at the Waldorf over on Summer Street, or the Auditorium on Andrew Street, all just a football throw from Central Square itself. Once in a while we would even meander into enemy territory, into West Lynn itself, the home of our hated rival Lynn Classical, to the Uptown Theater.

One final comment concerning movie magic in a young boy's life – the Auditorium was a very special place. On weekends we stood in the long lines which snaked along Andrew Street to catch a double bill from the smaller studios (Universal, Monogram, United Artists), both movies second run, but coupled with a serial such as "Spy Smasher," The Perils of Nyoka," "Captain Marvel," "Don Winslow of the Navy" and countless others, each fifteen episodes in length, about thirty minutes in duration, the hero or heroine left dangling from a cliff or from some crocodile's jaws from week to week. From Monday to Friday we wondered how our heroes could possibly survive such terrible encounters. But you know, they always did.

Unfortunately for us, from Monday through Friday, my friends and I had very little time for movies and for exploring the downtown. School beckoned, and Lynn being home to a large concentration of Catholics, many of us attended parochial schools. My parents enrolled me at St. Joseph's Institute in 1939. Located on Green Street just around the corner from Union Street and St. Joseph's Church itself, the school was a three-story red brick edifice next to a convent.

Because St. Joseph's Church was so close to our school, we were frequently marched, particularly on Fridays, to the church to make our confessions. Prisoners of war had more rights than we did. Woe be to the one, parading in columns of twos, who spoke on the march from Bataan – I mean the school – to the church. And once inside the lower church we dutifully awaited our turn to confess our sins and complete our penance. If you as much as smiled at the person to your right or left, you were asked to remain after school. And the Sisters of St. Joseph's weren't into teachers' rights, teachers' unions, or leaving the building three steps behind their charges. Staying after school meant anytime from a half-hour until 5:00 p.m., and with assigned duties such as washing blackboards and desks, cleaning erasers, and sweeping.

On Sunday itself we sat in the lower level of the church by grades, making it far easier for the nuns to a) take attendance mentally and b) easily identify probable culprits. Funny, in those less than democratic days, whether at the movies, at church, or at any place of public assembly, children were segregated from adults and relegated to the tough seats.

Above us, the Gothic cathedral built of red brick featured a steeple that hovered like a sentinel against the sky. The downstairs offered an ornate altar but everything else was reduced in scope in contrast with the beauty and sheer splendor of the second floor. There, row after row of oak pews greeted more than 2,000 parishioners who entered by way of three separate stairwells. Brightly lit, the interior overwhelmed the congregation. Dozens of chandeliers hung down from sloped, beautifully painted ceilings, and luminous windows composed of expensive stained glass ringed the two side aisles. Interspersed between the windows were depictions of the Stations of The Cross. At the center lay the sanctuary and the massive white marble altar that dominated the upstairs. Above the congregation, cathedral ceilings featured beckoning angels lifting young babies toward heaven.

On very special occasions – Confirmation, a marriage, a funeral – we were welcomed upstairs, but in the main the downstairs dominated our lives. And if for any reason (heart attack, bubonic plague) you missed Sunday Mass, then parents had to provide a Monday morning note for immediate presentation to Sister or expect a call home.

Our daily routine was set, arbitrary, and strictly adhered to. At exactly 8:15 a.m. we arrived at school and gathered with classmates adjacent to the convent or on the west side of the school. From within we would hear the sounds of a piano and a drum, played by one of the nuns or one of us, a signal to search out partners and parade in, not unlike Alec Guinness and his men in "Bridge on the River Kwai". Grades 1-3 proceeded to the first floor, grades 4-6 to the second, and grades 7-8 to the third.

In 1939 we left the building for lunch and raced home (no busses in those days) to mothers or grandmothers who were always there with soup, sandwiches, and comfort, unless you were carrying notes from Sister. On the way back, we might stop at Pop's variety store across from school if we had a penny for candy. By 1:30 p.m. we were back at our desks.

The Sisters of St. Joseph's were not child psychologists, decidedly not, but they were master teachers, particularly of the language arts. To this day I attribute my love of reading and writing to their superior teaching, to the hours they would spend on individual instruction. On the other hand, mathematics was learned very much by rote, as if the mastering of multiplication tables assured (it didn't) one's understanding of the underlying concepts. And science, as a subject, was unheard of. Everything in that realm was attributed to God. Darwin might as well never have existed. We, of course, studied religion as if we were Islamic fundamentalists in dire need of conversion. And all respect had to be rendered to the statuary to be found at various points in the classroom. Ask Stephen Rogers.

In 1942, when I moved to the fourth grade and the second floor, Stephen transferred to our school from a public school. I shall forever remember the mid-year day Stephen arrived, nervously sauntering through the classroom door, across the top of the room, forgetting to genuflect in front of the statue of the Virgin Mary. Sister Druscilla extended her personal welcome, dragging his form from his newfound seat and using him as a floor broom before depositing him in front of the Virgin where he remained kneeling for – I forget. He may still be there.

Dullards and/or wise guys were not tolerated. One day Sister Salvatore, my fifth grade teacher, asked my friend Arthur who was buried in Grant's tomb.

"Cary Grant," the nitwit replied.

"Cary Grant?" replied Sister Salvatore, a redness permeating the dark olive skin around her habit. "Is that what you said, Arthur?"

The nitwit thought he had guessed right. "Yes, Sister. Cary Grant."

Arthur had to write "I shall not be fresh to my teacher" three hundred times on the blackboard after school.

There was no such thing as a social promotion back in the early 40's. One of my best friends spent three years in the sixth grade and many others two years in a grade.

I was always glad I was an older brother, because, Lord forbid, you just didn't want to be a younger sibling. A constant with the Sisters was comparisons with family members who had preceded you. "Your brother Richard was a much smarter young man than you." "Your older sister Maureen wouldn't have failed this test." "Your older brother Gerald wouldn't have lice in his hair." For all I know Richard, Maureen, and Gerald could now be serving ten to fifteen at Walpole, but as I said earlier, the Sisters weren't exactly child psychologists.

And girls were considered angels compared to the boys. If someone stuck gum under a desk (a cardinal sin in those days), the girls were largely presumed innocent, quizzed with a smile, returned that smile demurely, while we boys were challenged through clenched teeth and threatened with corporal punishment.

Without the diversion of television, we read the classicists incessantly, outstanding writers such as Mark Twain, Robert Louis Stevenson, Herman Melville. We must have set world records for writing book reports, work that was scrutinized heavily by the Sisters to be sure we weren't plagiarizing from Classics Comics.

And we practiced penmanship each Monday and Friday, a lay expert teaching us the loops and curls and the side-saddle r's of the Palmer method. I wrote left-handed, close to a mortal sin in those days, with its connotation of one's sitting at the left hand of God. Those of us with this affliction had our left hands tied to our belts so we could learn the correct method. To this day, I can write with either hand. More importantly, we could all construct a whole sentence, diagram that sentence, and point out its parts of speech.

When we left eighth grade in 1947, those of us who transferred to public school had little problem with the adjustment. We were essentially prepared because our character and our values had been largely formed. I experienced some cultural shock, however, when I observed my ninth grade science teacher bouncing a young lady on his lap while providing a tutorial. My nuns would have strung him up by his – oh, never mind.

During the war (1941-1945), we were all united in our support of democracy against our axis enemies, particularly Germany and Japan. For the young, our responsibility was to sacrifice for the war effort by giving up on chocolate, standing in long lines at Blood's over on Silsbee Street to acquire butter through our family's rationing card and saving our pennies to buy stamps and bonds to support our military. I can still picture Bing Crosby singing "Won't you Buy a Bond for Freedom Today?"

Industrial Lynn boomed during those war years. Many of my neighbors worked at the General Electric Company, with many moms leaving homes for the very first time as "Rosie the Riveters" as the largest GE plant in the East churned out military hardware. Our soldiers and sailors would come home on leave occasionally, triggering block parties throughout the city neighborhoods in the support.

And who could ever forget August, 1945, the end of the war as Japan surrendered? I stood in Central Square underneath the overhead Boston & Maine train stop as confetti and rice rained over the center of the city and people streamed from the Waldorf Cafeteria, from Harold's Delicatessen, and from every point in the Square to celebrate our final victory, to hug and to kiss, our sense of togetherness making us feel life would always be this way. We would forever be in union with family, friends, neighborhood, and community.

And in the summer we had the ocean, allowing my city to temper its industrial nature and open up to its young all sorts of possibilities. As you come about the Nahant rotary, the first jewel in a crown of beaches comes into view. Lynn Beach stretches from a point a mile south of the rotary up toward Red Rock Park, a half-mile north. From there Kings Beach quickly appears on your right, its main feature Red Rock Park itself, a semi-circular indentation of green grass, walkways, and benches above the beach itself. At night it was and is the perfect spot for walkers and would-be lovers. Still a mile further north, just past the Lynn-Swampscott line, lies Fisherman's Beach, much smaller and much more intimate.

In the 40's families headed for Lynn Beach and its firmly-packed, expansive plain, a perfect place for tossing a tennis ball, for picnics, the beach only a short walk to Christie's Restaurant and a hot dog or a bottle of Coke pulled from a chest.

Those of us ten years of age, maybe a bit older, preferred King's Beach and its long seawall extending from Red Rock Park into Swampscott itself. Its huge waves pounded the sea wall at high tide. We would jump from stairwells into the undulating waves, being particularly careful not to hit the water when the waves were incoming for fear of being smashed against the wall itself.

At low tide we spread lunches of peanut butter sandwiches and bottles of Pepsi on to our towels, or we stood to bang tennis balls against the sea wall, chasing fly balls down into the surf with cries of "I'm Jimmy Piersall", or we played a game of "outs", seeing who could close down an inning with the fewest misses of ground balls bouncing from the wall to the sand.

As we grew into our teen years, we meandered into Swampscott, past Doane's Ice Cream Stand to the third jewel in the necklace – Fisherman's Beach, a relatively brief stretch of sand, frequented, though, by members of the opposite sex and by very few parents. There we would pour baby oil over dry bodies and savor the feeling, this being now the generation that used Ivory Soap for everything else – their once-a-week bath (no one had a shower), their hair shampoo (no wonder my hair was always itchy), and for general washing.

The Atlantic was our playground, and although the water temperature seldom reached 65 degrees until late July, we didn't care. We frolicked, sat in the sun for the whole day, (well-meaning mothers sent us off for the entire day with packed lunches and little concern about sun rays), and enjoyed our City of Firsts.

And we walked everywhere. Because we opened our homes to neighbors, because we lived in a simpler time, we walked the two miles to St. Joseph's and back home twice a day. We walked to Sam's sub shop up on

Lewis Street. We walked the six miles to the theaters – the Uptown, the Waldorf – over in West Lynn. We walked to Barry Park, six miles again, to watch Harry Agganis, Lynn's greatest athlete ever, play first base for Connery Post 6. We walked to Manning Bowl on a Friday night, football crowds of 15,000-23,000 post-war and pre-television gathering to watch strong English High teams and Harry Agganis's great Classical High teams play against dreaded invaders from Lowell, Lawrence, Haverhill, Salem, Peabody, Beverly, and Gloucester – all members of the original Essex County League.

When we played sports, we organized ourselves. In the 40's parents were advised to stop exercising at age thirty-five and remain sedentary so you never saw the kind of parental involvement you see today, the roaring loudmouths punching each other out at a hockey or Little League game.

For football we would just meet at some designated hour at one of the three or four designated places – the expansive Meadow, adjacent to English High School, large enough for five games to occur simultaneously;

an empty lot on Fayette Street next to my triple-decker home; the City Stables; Laundry Hill, above the B&M railroad tracks at the intersection of Fayette and Olive Streets; the Cook Street playground in the Highlands.

We wore no pads or helmets, largely because no one had any money to purchase them. I remember playing a tackle football game at Laundry Hill one day. Attempting to tackle my friend Ed Waldron, who would go on to become one of English's outstanding running backs, I tumbled over the flat ground down the embankment and onto the railroad tracks. I might as well have attempted to tackle a tank.

The organizers were the oldest or the toughest kids. Whatever the game, they also served as referees or umpires. Highly inflamed disputes were normally settled by fisticuffs if the rules interpreters were challenged. Sides were divided up by these same arbitrators so that those of us with few skills always had our feelings hurt by being assigned to center the ball in football, patrol right field in baseball, or wait for some starter to tire in basketball.

Occasionally we would travel – I mean walk – to face a Greek or Polish team at Barry Park or a neighborhood group at Clark Street or another gang of mainly Irishers up in the Highlands.

At night, except for the summer, we stayed home. The good Sisters believed in great gobs of homework, particularly Sister Salvatore, my fifth grade teacher, who wasn't happy unless you left the Institute carting six to eight books. But once that was done, under the watchful eyes of parents, who also did not stray far, you could look forward to gathering around the radio as a family to hear Jack Benny or the Lux Radio Theater, where movie stars would re-create their roles in currently available movies; or Fibber McKee and Molly, or The Great Gildersleeve. Occasionally the resonant, articulate voice of Franklin Delano Roosevelt would reach us over the airwaves, reporting to us regarding progress with the war effort, urging us to have faith. Unlike today, the President had few critics. He was our leader, our idol, the working class's best friend. And we were never told he was paralyzed. We never saw him as handicapped. On the contrary, news

John A. Curry

photos from conference sites such as Yalta would show him with a blanket about his legs. I just thought he was cold.

Whatever the season, our world was Lynn. It was practically unheard of for us to journey into Marblehead or Salem, maybe Nahant or Swampscott, but never Peabody or Beverly. We attended parochial school, and we lived parochially. We were largely taught to think parochially, particularly by our school. "Don't play with Protestants" we were warned. "Don't fraternize with Jews." "Don't ever enter a Protestant Church." We attended the only true church, we were told. I grew up thinking Protestants were Indians or at best second-rate citizens.

But we benefited greatly because life was simpler and largely black and white, and society agreed on what a young man and young woman should be exposed to, and the gradations and benchmarks for that exposure. In those days in the City of Firsts, we were greatly advantaged.

Of course, the proof always lies somewhere in the pudding. My good friends of the 40's, aided considerably by those institutions with which we interfaced, went on to distinctive careers in medicine (Dr. Art Boland); education (Dr. Jim Leonard, Lynn Superintendent of Schools; Peter Arslanian, principal, Lynn Classical High School), law (John McGloin); interior decorating (world famous decorator Carlton Varney); art (nationally known landscaper Robert Caulfield); business and finance (Bob McManus); law enforcement (Bill Mancinelli). I could go on and on.

Most definitely it was a glorious time to be young in the City of Firsts. In the 40's and in the conservative decade of the 50's that followed, we did not experience the tumultuous issues of the 60's and 70's – the civil rights movement, the push for women's rights, the growth and defeat of communism. The world, our country, and the City of Firsts all changed.

There's a line from a movie I saw in the fall of 1943 one Saturday afternoon in the dark at the Warner that sums up my feelings. Bogart turns to a never-more-radiant Bergman and tells her "We'll always have Paris."

Those of us privileged to have grown up in the City of Firsts will always have Lynn.

THE PASSENGER

"I caught the Celtics on the tube last night," said Gil Barnes, forty-eight, five-nine, stocky, studying the road behind them in the rearview.

"I don't watch anymore, not since they started shootin' three balls from three miles away," replied Fran Cassidy from the passenger seat of the stolen 2004 Cadillac. He was fifty-one, maybe five-seven, wiry, losing his hair.

"I shut it off after the first half," Gil Barnes was saying. "Larry Bird and Kevin McHale must have to take Prozac to watch the goings-on today – guys throwin' passes off the glass, guys nine foot tall missin' lay-ups, no one pushin' the ball up in transition..."

"First someone has to get the rebound before you can push it up," Fran Cassidy said.

"I blame M.L. Carr, Pitino, and Danny Ainge – three jokers posing as executives."

"Agreed. How do those ex-jocks get to be general manager anyway?"

"I'll tell you how," Gil said, shifting in his seat as they headed from Saugus into Lynn over on Walnut

Street. "Remember when we wuz kids growin' up? Every failed coach became a principal, not your best teachers mind you, but the coach whether he won or lost. Like maybe 98 percent of them became principals. It's like the Peter Principle."

"Peter Who? Who's he?"

"Shut up you moron."

"Why you keep lookin' in the rear mirror?"

Gil Barnes shrugged. "I won't feel comfortable until we unload the car, y'know? Anythin' can happen before we get it to the chop shop."

"It's a shame to cut up a '04 Caddy DeVille," Fran said.

"Not many of 'em get heisted, you know that?"

"What, Caddys?"

"Yeah. You know what the most stolen car is in the good old USA?"

"The Honda Accord?"

"Right on."

Gil Barnes pointed the sky blue DeVille toward the ocean, cutting across downtown Lynn, heading for Commercial Street and the chop shop.

"You watch the Super Bowl Sunday night?" he suddenly asked.

Fran Cassidy nodded. "I missed the halftime show, though."

"You didn't have to see it what with the networks and the locals showin' Jackson's tit eighty-five times all week long. Tagliabue says he's shocked," Barnes added, a ripple of laughter following.

"My ass!" Fran said. "Them and all the other pro leagues have been sellin' sex for years."

"They say it's entertainment."

"Why can't the ball game be entertainment enough?" Fran growled. "Look at the NBA. You go see the Celtics now and they got guys with slingshots shootin' underwear into the stands, monkeys shootin' baskets off a trampoline, fans wavin' their asses at the cameras…"

"Right. Like at the Super Bowl the other night. They're scared of terrorists, right? So first they scan everyone's ass lookin' for razor blades, but then at halftime they're shootin' off rockets and fireworks and shit from the stage itself! They're the terrorists! You know what I'd do if I wuz a terrorist, Fran? I'd join the band, y'know, one of them bands marchin' in at half-time? I'd dress up like one of them, I'd wear one of them costumes, hide some RX in my drum, and when the black broad starts flashin' her personals, I'd set off the bomb. Maybe take out 10,000 people before I go to heaven to meet twenty-four virgins. They got so much noise and light goin' on what's one more explosion? I'd just be considered part of the show."

"It was a wardrobe malfunction," Fran said.

"What was?"

"Jackson showin' her boob."

"If you believe that, I got a bridge I can sell you."

They crossed into the center of Lynn, onto North Common Street, Gil being sure to stay within the speed limit at all times.

"You hear somethin'?" Fran asked.

"What?"

"I don't know, like somethin' bumpin' maybe?"

"A flat?"

"No. More like from the trunk."

"Well, we're almost to the shop now."

"It's definitely the trunk," Fran said.

"I'll pull over."

Gil Barnes eased the Caddy into Magrane Square and found an empty spot between two SUV's big enough to launch aircraft. He cut the engine and handed the keys to Fran Cassidy.

Moving quickly, Fran hoisted the trunk and stood there staring for a long beat. Gil Barnes studied the uplifted trunk in the rearview for what seemed like an eternity. What was wrong?

Slamming down the trunk, Fran appeared on the driver's side signaling for Gil to lower the window. "What's the matter?" Gil asked, irritated.

"You're not goin' to believe this," Fran said, his breath forming huge puffs in the cold January night air.

"What?"

"There's a dead guy in the trunk!"

"You're shittin' me!"

"I ain't."

"Get the fuck out of the way so's I can open the door."

As Gil exited the Caddy, Fran looked about furtively and moved to pop the trunk once more.

"Look for yourself," he said.

"Jesus!"

Together they stared at an elderly man's forehead, the red spots from entry wounds in sharp contrast to his grayish hair. A black tarp covered most of his body.

"What the hell is this?" Gil asked, more to himself, not expecting any answer.

"I knew things was too easy here," Fran answered. "I mean some dork leaves his keys in the Caddy right over the visor."

Gil Barnes didn't respond. Instead, he lowered the tarp a bit.

"What are we gonna do? Stare at this stiff all night?" Fran asked in frustration.

"Look again, smartass."

"What?"

"Look at the face."

Fran Cassidy searched the eyes staring back at him. "Holy shit!"

"So the fuckin' dawn finally shines over Marble Head, huh?" Gil pointed to the body while, at the same time, he scanned the immediate area. No one was paying them much attention. About thirty yards away a battalion of teenagers, dressed in today's Omar the Tentmaker's fashions, clustered around the entrance to a convenience store.

"It's Mario 'The Gent' Gentilli!" Fran exclaimed.

"Correct. And not lookin' his best," Gil added.

"How the fuck did he get in here?"

"We gotta think is what we gotta do," Gil Barnes countered.

"Are we sure it's him?"

"There ain't been a day recently when his puss isn't plastered on page one of the papers, is there? The head of the Mafia in Boston, for Christ's sake. It's 'The Gent' no question."

"What'll we do?" Fran persisted.

"Somebody did him and left him right in the middle of the North Shore Shopping Mall parking lot," Gil said, trying to think it out, Fran not of much help, him with his brain fried half the time.

"And right in front of Barnes and Noble, too," Fran said.

Gil gave him his best Humphrey Bogart stare. "What the fuck's that got to do with anything?"

Fran shrugged his shoulder as Gil slammed the trunk down. "Nothing I guess. Maybe we should just bring him along to the chop shop?"

Gil shook his head. "Bernie's not there. He's flying out tonight. Stan's supposed to be there for the Caddy. Come on, let's drive a bit. I need to think."

As they headed toward Lynn Beach, Fran kept up a constant line of chatter. "We should bring him to the chop shop, Gil. Stan will know what to do. We shouldn't be ridin' around Lynn with him. We get stopped I'm back to Walpole for a life stretch and so ain't you. We're both three strikes-and-you're-out guys."

"If you'd shut up for a minute, I could think!" Gil screamed, pointing the Caddy toward the Nahant Rotary, thinking of driving up to Swampscott, the cops there on a Saturday night probably not worrying about two white guys driving through in a brand new DeVille.

"Bernie told us he wants the Caddy tonight, and we got it," Gil finally said. "We need to just dump the body somewheres and fast. So think. Where can we dump him?"

"Right here along the beach?" Fran blurted.

"Y'know, Fran, you gotta cut down on the coke. Your brain's fried. What are we gonna do?" he asked incredulously. "Waltz his ass down to the sea wall and plant him on a park bench?"

"I was just thinking…"

"No, you wasn't thinkin'. That's your problem. It's too public here."

"I got another idea."

"That's what I'm afraid of."

"No. I mean it. How about we go back to Lynn, drop his ass out behind some school, maybe like Breed over on O'Callaghan Way."

Gil didn't answer.

"What's wrong with that?" Fran asked.

"It's too private," Gil finally said. "The cops could notice a car behind a school in that neighborhood."

John A. Curry

Fran thought on it as they entered Swampscott, the hills looking like a child's gingerbread cake at night. Gil turned over Walker Road heading down to Paradise Road, trying to decide whether to turn back toward Lynn.

"How about Lynn Woods?" he finally asked, more to himself than to Fran.

"Yeah!"

"Just 'yeah' is that all you got to say?"

"What do you want me to say?"

"Say it's a brilliant idea because that's what it is. Once we're in the woods themselves, we're not gonna bump into some cops. Who the fuck goes into the Lynn Woods on a cold winter night? We go in a couple of miles off the main road, toss the Gent under some fuckin' bushes, and get out of there quickly. Then we bring the car to Stan. What do you think?"

"Yeah."

"Yeah? That's all you think? You know the more I think about it the more I think I ought to take out my Sig Sauer, plant three or four in you, and leave you and

90

the Gent vegetating together under the same fuckin' tree."

Fran decided not to say "yeah" again.

Gil eased the Caddy back into Lynn, staying within the speed limit, darkness permeating everything, the lamp posts on the city streets providing about as much light as a candlestick.

They cruised through Wyoma Square and headed into the woods at a point practically across the street from Briarcliff Lodge on Great Woods Road. At exactly ten o'clock they entered the woods itself, the area five miles in length and three across. Easing up on the accelerator, Gil stayed on the dirt road for a distance of a mile before it narrowed to an impassable pathway.

"What we do is lug his ass up that hill, past those trees, and cut out of here fast," Gil was saying, pointing to his right.

"Who would ice the Gent?" Fran asked, his brain still back in Swampscott.

"We did as far as anyone who comes along here is concerned so let's get it done," Gil said, cutting the motor, exiting the car.

In the distance, a baying howl carried itself in the wind. "What the fuck's that?" Fran asked.

"Some coyote or wolf probably," Gil replied hesitantly. "Let's unload the Gent," he said.

Opening the trunk they lifted the Gent by utilizing the tarp wrapped about him.

"He's not bleeding out," Fran offered.

"Thank God for small favors."

Grunting, Gil nodded toward the hill to their right. "Let's do it."

They ascended the hill, walking through mush and mud along the winding path. "Toss his ass on the top of this rise under that tree over there," Gil ordered.

"The prick must weigh three hundred pounds," Fran said.

They dropped the Gent unceremoniously under a giant oak tree.

"What's that noise?" Fran asked suspiciously.

"What noise?"

"Somethin'. I heard somethin'."

Suddenly from the bottom of the hill something charged through the clearing, racing uphill through the underbrush, snapping branches in the process. Quickly, Fran reached for his clip holster and drew out his seven-shot Heckler and Koch as the form ran away from them, about twenty yards to their right.

As the noise increased, Fran let off a fusillade of bullets, emptying the clip. With a loud thud, the form collapsed behind a string of pine trees and mulberry bushes, sounding like an earthquake as it fell.

"What the fuck you doin?" Gil screamed.

"It's a friggin' grizzly is what – coming right at us," Fran yelled, his fear hanging there in the air.

"Jesus! You might as well wake up half of Lynn!" Gil replied, heading toward the pine trees, glancing down at the form.

"It's a deer. You shot a deer!" he said derisively.

Fran shrugged his shoulders. "The fucker was chargin' right at us," he said defensively.

Gil emitted a huge sigh. "We scared him more than he scared us. He was just tryin' to avoid us, you dummy!"

"So what's the big deal?"

"What's the big deal? Is that what you said? With them new environmental laws we'll do more time for shootin' the deer than if we had whacked the Gent."

"Huh?"

"You ever watch the news, Fran?"

"I watch Howard Stern."

"That figures. Practically every night on TV they show some god damn whale on a beach with ninety-five veterinarians tryin' to hoist his fat ass back into the drink. Then just the other day in Boston some gorilla named Little Joe escaped from the Franklin Park Zoo. Must have been fifty cops chasin' his mangy butt all around Dorchester, instead of just cappin' the fucker on the spot. And did you ever see one of them seals get beached? When they do, an army of people, all of them workin' overtime, all of them raisin' our taxes, are throwin' lassos around him to throw his balls back in the briny so's some shark can have him for supper. The deer's more problem than the Gent."

Suddenly Gil's phone chirped. "Now what?" he sighed. "We stay here any longer we might as well order Domino's."

"Gil? This is Bernie. Where are you?"

Gil looked puzzled. "Bernie? Where are you?"

"At the airport. Waitin' to clear security for the flight to Miami. I'm in a line goes back to Southie practically. There's a guy three or four ahead of me right now they got stripped to his under drawers. Pretty soon we'll all be flying naked."

He lowered his voice. "You guys cop the Caddy? Stan tells me you ain't arrived yet. Where the fuck are you?"

"There's been a complication, Bernie."

"Am I gonna find out where you are sometime tonight?"

"In the woods. Lynn Woods."

Bernie let that hang in the air for a few minutes. "What?" he finally said.

"There's a problem. We scooped the Caddy over at the mall. When we opened the trunk, we found a body – a cold one – in there so we're dumping it in the woods," Gil said. "Then we'll bring the car to Stan."

"Let me get this straight. You guys are wanderin' around in Lynn Woods with a stolen Caddy and a dead body?"

"Correct," Gil said. "And not just any body, Bernie. You know the guy."

"I know the guy! How would I know the guy?"

"Everybody in our business knows the guy. It's Mario Gentelli."

Bernie didn't say anything right away. "You guys stole a car with the Gent's body in it? Someone iced the Gent?"

"Now you got it," Gil affirmed.

"Tell him we got some other complications," Fran interjected.

"What's he sayin'?" Bernie asked.

"Nothing. We had to shoot a deer, too."

Bernie practically screamed into the cell. "Listen to me, you two morons. I don't want a car that's had the head of the Mafia's dead body in it. Leave the body, leave the car, and get the fuck out of there." He paused. "What's he sayin?"

"Nothing," Gil replied. "Fran was just wonderin' how we get home is all. Hello? Hello? He hung up."

"All this trouble, and he don't want the Caddy?"

Gil placed the cell in his jacket pocket. "He's pissed. Come on, we're leaving. And let's toss the guns somewhere off the path on our way out. Somewheres where they won't be found. We don't need some cop stoppin' us on the walk to Wyoma Square."

"We gotta walk?"

"What you want me to do? Call a taxi and like say, 'Excuse me, Town Taxi. Could you pick me up in Lynn Woods where me and the moron just dumped Mario the Gent? We'll be two miles in – look for a stolen Caddy or a deer with his balls reamed with seven-shot?' 'Of course, we gotta walk!'"

They turned away from the Caddy and headed back toward the entrance along a narrow trail. Above them the full moon was traversed by a string of clouds, moving slowly, like a locomotive on a straight line.

"And what are we gonna say if some cop does stop us?" asked Fran. "I mean it's almost a mile walk to Wyoma Square after we get out of here."

"We just say we're two guys out for a constitutional," Gil replied. "Besides they could give a shit about walkers. You could be marchin' to Georgia balleky ass and they'd drive on by. They're lookin' for kids this time of night – some kids racin' around in their Grand Am's."

"We could heist another car," Fran offered.

"No thank you. We've had enough passengers for one night. Like the broad said in 'Gone With the Wind' – "Tomorrow is another day."

"Was she in the rackets?"

"Fran, just walk and shut the fuck up."

HOME INVASION

Roberto looked at his street-market Rolex, sipping on the Pepsi can, trying to look cool, his pants practically dragging in the mud as he crossed Hood Park in Lynn, heading back toward Curwin Circle.

"We need to acquire some more product," he said to Luis, the two of them seventeen years old going on forty.

"And how you gonna get that?" Luis asked in his blue and white Tommy jacket and black do-rag, wearing the same blousy cargo pants as Roberto, the same vacant stare that made them as rock-heads.

"We first needs cash," Roberto surmised.

"And how you gonna get that?"

"What are you – a fuckin' tape recording?"

Luis flinched. No need to rile Roberto so he stayed quiet.

"What we do is go on over to one of them side streets off Boston Street – maybe Starratt Street, knock on the door of one of them cottages and say 'Good evening. Your money or your life'."

"You mean like trick or treat?"

Roberto tossed him a look, wondering whether he was being dis'd or whether Luis was just reinforcing the fact that he had spent six years in the three-year middle school up at Pickering.

"Yeah, like trick or treat," he finally responded, giving Luis the benefit. "We might even use them words."

Luis thought on it for a beat. "You got the Beretta with you?"

"Of course. I don't go nowhere without my fifteen loads."

"Why don't we just go over to one of the convenience stores on Boston Street, shove the Beretta in some honky's face?"

Roberto shook his head vigorously. "That's old world shit. We's modern age mothers. You go in the convenience store now they got surveillance cameras takin' shots of your ass and Asians now all runnin' the stores rather die than let you get away with ten bucks. No, that shit's for losers."

"So why's a house better?"

"You know, Luis, you gotta start thinkin' for yourself. Maybe I ain't always gonna be around here once I get some money. I'll buy me a car with tight rims, be heading maybe for Miami or Kissimmee.."

"Where?"

"Where what?"

"Kissimmee?"

"A city, you dumb dork. A city in Florida. Down there they say call it Kissimmee by day, but Kiss-i-me at night. Get it?"

Luis nodded, even though he didn't know what Roberto was talkin' about.

"A house is way better to score," Roberto was saying. "First of all, most of them around here don't have cameras – these aren't estates you know, just average to above average homes. We find one has a car like a Grand Marquis in the driveway."

"A Grand Marquis?"

"Only ones drive a Grand Marquis or a Lincoln LS is old people. And that's what we want. We go to a house, find some old guy or woman or both, scare the shit out of them with the Beretta, tell them to come up with the cash. They'll shit their pants, tell us some half-truth, maybe give us some money but then we tie them up, spend the rest of the night searchin' the whole house. It's perfect."

"It sounds good."

"That's the first positive thing you've said tonight. Of course it's good. We dealin' with decrepits, and we got plenty of time once we're in the house."

"What if someone sees us knockin' at the door?"

"All these houses around here? First of all it's dark and we be smart to find a house sort of protected from some asshole's nosey eyes."

"I don't want to hurt no old people," Luis said.

"Maybe all we do is bitch-slap them around," Roberto lied. "I'll handle it you don't have the balls."

"I can bitch-slap upside the head."

"Good. I'm glad you can do somethin' help us along. We's home invaders tonight, Luis. You just follow my lead, and after a couple of scores like this we'll be headin' to the sun, find us some women wearin' those thongs, get us some blow whenever we want it, we be leadin' the high life."

—

Gertrude Halloran sat there staring at the tube without really seeing anything. What was there to see anyway? At eight o'clock she could watch Bill O'Reilly claiming, like he did every night, that he told it like it is, with no spin, the guy never saying anything good about any Democrat, or she could switch to the network movie, truncated by forty minutes of advertising per sixty minutes. Or maybe she could just go to bed and listen to Michael Savage on talk radio, he playing "The Mexican Hat Dance" repeatedly to show his disdain for Bush's new immigration policy. The loudmouth was aptly named, Gertrude thought.

For tonight and every night, her choices were limited. She was virtually alone with no one to really speak to. She really didn't count Russell even though he was only fifteen feet away, sitting there in his leather chair, only sixty years old but looking like eighty, the Alzheimer's having stripped him of his dignity as well as most of his mind.

She searched out her one glass of VO and ginger and rolled the ice about the glass. She was careful not to abuse her one treat, but more and more she looked forward each night to the amber, to its heady effect.

Russell gurgled ever so slightly as he stared straight ahead at O'Reilly, not understanding a word about the bullshit of how Clinton had caused the current economic woes, not Bush, the guy having been in office now almost four years yet still responsible for nothing, according to O'Reilly.

Looking at Russell these days always drove her thoughts to memories of the past, to the days he had courted her, days when his stringy white hair had been Irish ebony and his now fissured face as smooth as silk, the chin dimpled and clean shaven.

When she had first met him, he had been a school teacher right here in Lynn over at Ingalls Elementary and she a science teacher at English High. They met at a retirement party for a principal who had served at both schools. At six foot, rangy, looking like an Adonis, he had swept her off her feet first asking her to dance, then offering to take her home. For weeks after that they had taken long walks together along Lynn Beach Boulevard, getting to know one another, sharing mutual interests such as movies, politics, sports.

One night, maybe three months after they had first met, they were dining at Ruth's Restaurant behind the Warner Theater when he proposed to her, offering the ring across the table in that diffident way of his. She had found him then, as she did now some forty years later, a man without pretensions, a contented largely un-ambitious everyman who lived for his profession and his students.

Funny. In contrast, from an early age she had reeked of ambition. She just had to place first in elementary school, had graduated from St. Mary's as a valedictorian, earned a full scholarship to Boston College, where she finished third in her class. Later, much later, after they had married, she had moved rapidly from her position as teacher to assistant to full principal at English – its first woman principal, and one on the fast track to the superintendency.

Their love was strong and endearing, yet she had insisted there would be no children, nothing to deter her career ambitions. A stupid mistake in retrospect, particularly recognizable after she had fallen ill with breast cancer ten years ago.

The illness had derailed her career for a time, but it had brought them even closer together, Russell there for her each step of the way – through the initial diagnosis, the biopsy, the mastectomy, the treatments. And it was he who urged her back on the career path, rekindling her aspiration, subjugating his own needs. Just three years ago she had been elected superintendent of schools. And then he was forever beside her at holiday functions, school socials, smiling proudly her way despite his oft times being neglected or designated as "the super's spouse" by the hangers-on, the mean-spirited ones.

It was at one of the school functions — a retirement party at Lynn Woods School – that she first noted his problem. He had tugged at her sleeve and when he gained her attention he surprised her.

"Who's the lady in the red hat?" he had asked, pointing to the business agent for the school system, a woman he had known for years.

"You're kidding," Gertrude had replied.

"Who is she?"

"You don't know Catherine Carlson?"

"Oh, yes. Of course. I must be getting old," he had laughed.

Granted from there the deterioration had been gradual, but it had also been progressive. In just a two-year span his short-term memory loss escalated, causing Russell to seek early retirement only a year ago.

A few months ago she had begrudgingly joined him in retirement, two years ahead of her own personal schedule, and now, as he sat there focusing on everything and nothing she tried, as usual, to bury a small measure of resentment.

But she was ashamed as well, aware by her own selfishness and self-centeredness in not thinking first of the man who had always put her first. But she was here, wasn't she? She had chosen to be with him, hadn't she?

It was the loneliness that bothered her. Russell communicated only sparingly now, and often would spend a whole day without uttering even a word. Soon she would need to place him in a home, but something inside her – love, loyalty, gratitude, whatever – told her they were not yet ready to depend on the kindness of strangers.

—

Roberto and Luis hung back in the shadows as they picked their way down Starratt Road, searching out the dimly lit cottages, noting the car models adjacent to each home.

"There's a fool with a Lincoln LS," said Luis, pointing out a driveway at the very end of the street.

"Let's walk right by. We'll circle the block. Come right back here. You see that cottage across the street from us?"

"Yeah?"

"What I'm doin' is what they do in the army," said Roberto. "I'm reconnoitering."

"Recon what?"

Roberto bitch-slapped him on his shoulder. "Luis, you as dumb as shit. No wonder you in the alternative school."

"You there too!"

Roberto nodded. "My choice, fried brains. I use it as my base of operations. You know, for chicks, hash, shit like that." He paused for a moment. "Reconnoitering is like sneakin' around before we move. Be sure no citizens around. Be sure we's not bothered when we invade the house. We military we got to act like military. Speaking of which, in this here army I the general and you the recruit. So pay attention and be ready when I say so."

Luis considered that. "I in the army, but I got no weapon."

"That's cause you probably shoot yourself in the ass," Roberto countered. "Come on. We gonna circle the terrain."

Luis didn't dare ask what terrain meant.

—

At first Gertrude wasn't quite sure she heard it, not with Fox's other house conservative, Sean Hanitty, trying to prevent his liberal partner Alan Colmes from getting a word in edgewise. They were arguing about gays, Hanitty not willing to give them a seat on the bus, testing her own liberal sensibilities.

And then she heard it again. A sound like the doorknob rattling or being tampered with. She stood and walked to the huge picture window, and ever so slightly pulled aside the custom-made curtain. On the front steps stood two young boys, the one dressed in a bomber jacket now knocking lightly on the door.

She thought on them for just a moment, quickly determining that she would not respond to the knocking or the bell ringing now accompanying it. She looked across at Russell who sat now a bit more upright, not because of the ringing but because he was busily engaged in switching the stations, moving through the channels so rapidly there was no way he could be absorbing their content.

Deciding that if she remained quiet they would soon disappear, Gertrude moved away from the window back toward her seat.

—

"They saw us. Someone was at the window," Luis said excitedly. "Let's split."

Roberto was still talking his military bullshit. "We're gonna stick to our objective. It's quiet here. No one's around."

He knocked a bit more forcefully on the door. "Excuse me. Could someone help us please?" he said in a high-toned pitch. "Our car broke down. Could we use your phone?"

—

Gertrude Halloran hadn't gotten elected superintendent of schools because her mother had raised stupid children. She still didn't respond. On the other hand, she didn't think to call 911 either. The boys probably had broken down, but if they had why hadn't they called for help on a cell? In 2004 every kid from 10-18 was running up $200 monthly bills calling some other kid in Cancun so what was with these guys?

Standing, she felt herself tense. Her natural inclination was to help those in need, and more and more these days, she missed communicating with others. Since her retirement – no, since Russell's retirement – friends didn't call much anymore. She had left a position where she had been surrounded by people, complementing her natural gregariousness, for a life that was now both sedate and lonely.

Moving quietly, she stood a few yards from the front door. "I'm sorry. I'm alone," she found herself blurting out. "I can't help you."

Outside, Roberto nodded aggressively at Luis. "You hear that?" he whispered.

"Lady, could you just let us use your cell for a minute! I can call my friend to come get us. Would that be okay?" Roberto asked in his smooth, charming way.

"Wait a minute," came the voice from within.

Within seconds a tall, lanky woman, maybe sixty-five years old, her face only half showing, opened the door a few inches and stared at them across the chain. "Here. You can use this," she said passing the Nokia.

Without replying, Roberto shoved hard against the door, splitting the latch from the frame, the Nokia falling to the mat as he entered. Behind him, Luis scanned the neighborhood for any sign of trouble. Other than the sound of the northeast wind whistling through the trees, he didn't hear or see a thing.

Directly in front of him, Roberto was pushing the skanky old broad across the room threatening her with the Beretta. "Shut the fuck up!" he was hissing as he steered her toward a seat on the couch.

"Get out of my house!" Gertrude replied, raising her arms to protect her face as Roberto slapped her hard.

She fell onto the couch, sobbing now, as Roberto looked around, focusing on Russell who stared straight ahead at the tube. "What's his problem?" Roberto asked.

"You leave him alone! He has Alzheimer's. He's a very sick man!" Gertrude yelled.

"Hey! Old man! On your feet and get over here to the couch!" Roberto commanded.

Russell continued to watch the basketball game.

Quickly Roberto crossed the room and placed the Beretta against Russell's' temple. "Listen to me, old man. When I tell you to haul ass, you haul ass. You understand, you bag of shit?"

Russell stared straight ahead at the ball game.

"Leave him alone!" Gertrude screamed.

Russell finally looked at Roberto. "Hello," he said.

"Hello? Is that what you got to say?"

"He doesn't understand you!" Gertrude pleaded.

Roberto mulled it over. "Luis, go out in the kitchen or down cellar and find some tape or something to tie his dead ass with," he commanded.

"What do you want?" Gertrude asked more quietly now.

Roberto turned to face her. "We's home invaders. What we want is money, jewelry, shit like that. You don't want to see the dead dude's head bashed open, you best find some for me."

Gertrude rubbed the red welt forming next to her eye. "We don't keep much cash around the house. I have a little but.."

"Where is it?" he asked as Luis returned with a strand of rope.

"Tie his ass down and tape his mouth," Roberto directed.

"I have some in my pocketbook over there," she said "Next to the television."

Quickly Roberto snatched it and rifled through its contents. "Thirty bucks," he snickered. "What else you got in here?"

As Luis looped the rope about the easy chair, Gertrude considered her options and responses. First of all, they were doing her a favor tying Russell down. Most times in the evening he was relatively immobile, but she never knew when he might decide to wander, to move about. Under these circumstances they would focus less on him once he was tied. Secondly, she needed to think on how she could protect the man who had loved and cared for her over forty years. There was absolutely no guarantee that these obviously coked-out teens wouldn't murder them both once their search was completed.

"I have some jewelry upstairs," she finally replied. "And a little more cash," she added.

Roberto pointed at her with the Beretta. "On your feet, skank. Luis, you watch the zombie and check out the window every few minutes. And look around downstairs here, see what we can cop."

"Like Roberto, what am I lookin' for?" Luis asked.

"Remember what I told you about when the general give an order?"

Luis flinched and held out his hands palms up. "I just want to know what I'm lookin' for is all."

"Stupid shit. I ought to clock you right now," the general replied as he grabbed Gertrude's elbow and pushed her ahead of him up the stairs.

—

She thought it through as they ascended the spiral staircase. The danger was with her. Not only did Roberto have the weapon, but he was more vicious and more intelligent than the boy called Luis. For one thing, Luis never flashed a weapon of any type. He appeared to be unarmed. He seemed more a hanger-on, a worshipper of a false god, rather than a imminent threat.

Maybe.

She sensed Roberto's intent. He would scour the house for any valuables they could carry and, in all probability, kill her and Russell before leaving. Why else had he referred to Luis by name? Why else had he not recoiled when Luis called him by name?

Her chance to act was now fast approaching, and that window of opportunity would soon close. As soon as she provided Roberto with information regarding the location of her valuables, he would bring her back downstairs, strap her to a chair as well, and then ransack the house more completely. And in the end there was a distinct possibility he would kill them.

At the top of the stairwell, Roberto pressed the Beretta into the small of her back. "Which room?" he asked excitedly.

"Over here," she said, pointing directly across the hall to their bedroom.

Shoving her ahead, he scanned the room. A huge Queen-sized bed was covered with an afghan quilt and surrounded on one side by a dresser and on the other by a chest of drawers. In one corner a closet was fronted by sliding doors.

"Where's the stuff?" he demanded.

Gertrude readied herself, counting slowly from ten back down to one, calming herself. "There's a jewelry box in the chest of drawers and some money up high in a shoe box in the closet."

Roberto grinned in anticipation. "So far you're doin' all right, grandma. Now you go get me the jewelry first. Bring me the box."

She knew what she had to do, the trick was in the actual action. David Copperfield always talked about the importance of diversion, of stealth, of letting the observer believe his eyes have not betrayed him, of creating an illusion. Could she palm the scissors while both picking up the jewelry box and handing it across to him? She could if she could get him to concentrate on the jewels themselves.

Moving to the chest, she opened the top drawer and lifted the long square box out slowly, gripping the scissors against the bottom of the box. Turning slowly to him, she opened the box with her left hand holding the scissors firmly with her right.

"Jesus! You must be rich, lady!" Roberto exclaimed, focusing entirely on the box contents. As he reached for the box, she slid her right hand along the seam of her nightgown, dropping the scissors into the long pocket on her right side.

For a moment he paid her no particular attention as his eyes swept over the various pieces. Then, in a quick movement, he placed the box on the bed and stared at her. "And the cash?"

"It's on the shelf up there," she replied evenly.

"Get it."

"I can't reach it without the stair step downstairs," she replied.

"Fuck that."

He turned to the closet, opened it, and studied the area. On a shelf three feet above him the shoe box lay on top of four or five other boxes.

Paying her little attention, Roberto reached for the box, standing on his toes so that when the scissors entered his spinal cord he simply deflated, falling forward into the wall, gasping for final breath.

"What the hell's goin' on up there?" Luis yelled from below.

"We'll be right down!" she exclaimed.

She picked up the Beretta and examined it. She knew very little about guns, but she could see the safety catch was off and in all probability Roberto had one ready in the chamber.

Moving quietly out of the bedroom, she paused at the top of the stairwell to gather her bearings, to try and calm her racing heart. She could hear Russell stuggling, breathing hard, trying to speak despite the tape covering his mouth.

Descending slowing, she listened intensely for any sign divulging the whereabouts of Luis. She kept the Beretta close to her body as she entered the living room.

Sitting aside of Russell, Luis was watching a Road Runner cartoon, his eyes completely focused on the tube. When he sensed her presence, he looked up, confused.

"Where's Roberto"? he asked, starting to rise.

She raised the Beretta so that he could see it. "Get out of my house!" she screamed.

Luis took off as if he were in a race with the Road Runner himself. Bolting straight ahead, he slammed the door behind him and ran down the steps.

Hesitatingly, Gertrude approached Russell and gently tugged at the tape covering his mouth. Quickly she pulled it away, causing him to cry aloud, showing his disorientation.

"What is happening?" he sobbed, half hysterical.

"Everything is fine, now, Russell," she said, soothingly, releasing his bonds.

"I'm tired," he said.

"Come, dear. Lie down on the couch while I just make a call. Then we'll get ready for bed."

He didn't respond, but followed her to the couch and lay down, a smile now crossing his face. "I can see the television from here," he said.

Suddenly a frown creased his forehead. "Who were those boys?" he asked as she dialed 911.

"Nothing for you to worry about, dear," she replied calmly. "Just some boys come to visit us."

PAYING OFF THE DEBT

Jack Kelly scanned the platform at South Station once again as the conductor yelled out his last "All aboard" call. He checked his watch – 8:00. Jerry had said he would be here by 7:30. On the last Saturday in November 1955, snow was just beginning to fall, and the forecast for six to ten inches by afternoon did not bode well for their trip to New Haven. Suddenly, he spotted Jerry running down the platform toward him. "Drop in anytime," Jack said, as they climbed aboard about a minute before departure.

Despite the weather and the hour, the train was packed with revelers, almost all of them Jerry's age, talking loudly, poking at one another, slipping flasks to their friends from under heavy overcoats. About a quarter of them were young women, fresh faced and buoyant, dressed for the weather in long winter coats and crimson hats.

"Nice quiet people you hang around with, Jerry," Jack said, removing his blue topcoat before an overly zealous son of Harvard noticed its color.

"Come on, big brother, don't be a killjoy. You love football. I remember you zigzagging all over Laundry Hill – all that action and you kept me on the sidelines," Jerry laughed.

Jack recalled the tackle football games the brothers and their friends had played above the railroad tracks back in the 40's. Until he was ten, Jack refused to let Jerry do anything but referee or chase down and spot the ball. "We didn't like playing on a day like this, kid. I hope some of you Harvards brought snowplows to clear the field for that old-fashioned single wing shit you run," Jack said.

"Don't be so negative. Yale's light and fast this year, so maybe the snowfall will help us."

The snow thickened as they headed west, the slow New York-bound train chugging its way through Newton, Framingham, and Worcester. Strong northwest winds whipped the snowflakes against the window, making it nearly impossible to see outside. He turned to look at the handsome freshman sitting next to him. "So how's the first year going, Jerry?"

Jerry paused, giving Jack a few seconds to study close up the changes in his brother. If anything, he was even more handsome. At eighteen, his lanky frame resembled Jack's, in contrast to their brother Tommy's smaller, more compact build. The matted black hair, parted on the left, the broad forehead with elongated black eyebrows above beautiful blue eyes, and the straight nose so characteristic of the Irish made him more beautiful than handsome. Whether at Fisherman's Beach or on this train, Jack had seen young women staring at him.

"How's Marjorie doing, Jack?"

"Fine. But I asked you about school," Jack insisted.

"I love it. The professors are absolutely first-rate. They challenge you to think, to be critical, to reflect before answering," Jerry enthused. "Some of the best minds in the world teach you to look at the big picture."

"How're you doing?"

"It's hard to know, Jack, but I think I'm holding my own. You know, Lynn English was great preparation for Harvard. I had good teachers who insisted we earn our grades. Yeah, I'm doing fine so far. I'll know more after first semester exams. But whatever happens, I owe it to you, Jack."

Jack tapped him on the arm. "You owe me nothing, kid. You've earned your way, all the way. I'm only helping the way Ma would have expected me to. To take care of you, the way she took care of us. No problems, then?"

Jerry shook his head almost too quickly, Jack thought, and then, again, turned the conversation back to Jack.

"So now…what about Marjorie? What's going on between you two?"

Jack smiled, thinking of the past summer and of his growing closeness to Marjorie. Now that he was working for her father, he saw her constantly. They dated only each other, and he found himself always looking forward to the next time he would be with her. They were friends, confidants, eager young lovers totally absorbed in each other.

He grimaced, contemplating for the moment the lie he was living. In the evenings, after 9 p.m., he would use the excuse of homework for the two courses he was taking at Northeastern on Saturday mornings to drop her off. From Jimmy Flaherty's point of view, all was perfect. Jack now had a legitimate, less physical job, which left plenty of time for crime family activities in the evenings. Over lunch at Dini's on Tremont Street one recent day, Jimmy had once again stressed the importance of legitimate enterprises for all family members and reiterated his insistence that the members live comfortably but never ostentatiously.

"It's important to live and look legit. Deal only in cash. No checks, no charge cards, nothing but cash. Charge cards are for suckers. And keep the cash out of the banks as much as you can. Stash it in some safe haven. Forsake the interest. Don't be piggish. If the cops ever ask where you got such an accumulation, then tell 'em the ponies at Suffolk or from those asshole dogs chasing the white rabbit at Wonderland. Whatever, be smart. Nothing in writing. Deal in cash, and be ready to show a pay stub for a good week's work."

The train lumbered along the track, moving more slowly than usual and usual meant moving with glacial speed. "She's doing fine. We're very serious about each other. She's kind, considerate – she hasn't allowed her father's success to spoil her." He paused for a moment. "Jerry, I gave her a friendship ring last week."

Grabbing his hand, Jerry pumped it vigorously. "Well, big brother, you finally got smart. You don't deserve her. I'm happy for you." Although the words were sincerely stated, Jack couldn't help but notice the worried look in his eyes.

"Jerry, what's the problem?" Jack asked. "Something's bothering you."

"Aah, I guess I need to ask you for a loan, Jack. I need some cash," he stammered.

"Hey, little guy, that's okay. What? $25? $50? Will that do it?"

"Jack, I'm in some deep trouble. I need $5,000."

$5,000! Jack almost jumped from his seat. "You're shitting me!"

"Jack, I'm ashamed to even ask you. But I need your help. Do you have that kind of cash?" he asked anxiously.

Jack stared at his brother before answering. "Let's go back to square one. Why do you need that kind of money?"

Jerry fidgeted in the seat, looking at the window, the landscape now barely visible in the driving storm. "This fall I started betting on football games, using the expense money you sent with the tuition. Just little bets to begin — $5.00, $10.00 – no more. I had some early success so I doubled to $10.00 and $20.00 bets. Before I knew it, I was in the hole for $300."

"That's a long way from $5,000. What the hell happened?" Jack asked.

"This bookie I placed bets with – Ferdie Gallipoli – carried me for a while and then loaned me the money to pay the original debt. Later on, he surprised me. He says I owe him the vig on the debt, and the vig goes up each day I don't pay. I had no money to pay him, vig or no." Jerry's voice climbed an octave as he spoke.

"How much did you actually lose?" Jack asked.

"About $500," Jerry replied. "But there's something else, Jack. This guy Gallipoli means business."

"What do you mean?"

"Last Monday night I was walking near the campus on the way back from Harvard Stadium after watching the frosh practice. I was alone. Gallipoli and two of his heavyweights stopped me." He rolled back his sweater and revealed his left arm. A long knife slash extended from his wrist to his elbow, the cut skillfully sewn together with a number of stitches.

Jack stared at the wound, his lips thinning, his face grim. "Who did this to you? Which one?" he asked.

"Gallipoli slashed me. Said it was a warning. If I don't have the $5,000 by next Saturday, he says I won't be seeing many more Saturdays after that," Jerry replied nervously. "Can you help me, Jack? Jesus, I don't know how I can even ask you, but I don't know where else to turn."

Looking at the arm, Jack thought back to the time when Jerry had been vaccinated. He must have been four or five years old when Jack has asked to take him on his tricycle to Goldfish Pond. "All right," their mother had agreed, "but be sure he doesn't get wet." Before Jack knew it, Jerry, pedaling down the steep embankment that led to the edge of the pond, had plunged into two feet of water. There had been no problem getting him out, but Jack would always remember his failure to protect Jerry and his mother's disappointment in him.

"New Haven, next stop," the conductor bellowed.

Jack carefully pulled the sweater down over Jerry's arm. "Jerry, you never worry about asking me for anything, you understand? I'm your brother, and your problems are my problems. Where can I find this guy Gallipoli?"

"Jack, if you can give me the money now, I'll pay you back, and soon. I can get a job as a waiter and .."

"Look, kid. There's going to be no waiting on tables. You just study and pay attention to those grades. I'll worry about finances, and you can repay me when you graduate. Deal?" he said, extending his hand.

"Okay, Jack. I don't know what to say."

"Say nothing. I'll see him before next Saturday and take care of the debt. You keep away from him now and forever. You understand? Now where do I find him?"

The train slowed as they entered New Haven Station. Along with hundreds of others, they walked the mile and a half to Yale Bowl, the storm intensifying by the minute. Blue clad Yalies yelled light insults at Harvards as they drove by, half of them swerving just enough to toss slush from the tires in their direction.

At the Bowl, over 70,000 fans, undaunted by the weather, huddled in the cavernous old structure, fueled both by the excitement of the great rivalry and by the flasks they raised more than occasionally to their lips. For over three hours the teams battled, with the superior ground game of the Bulldogs leading them to a 21-7 victory, the only Harvard touchdown coming in the fading minutes of the contest on a five yard pass to Teddy Kennedy, a senior end from Hyannisport, Massachusetts.

—

Ferdie Gallipoli sat in his backroom office late Saturday morning counting the night's take, keenly anticipating the rush of action on this afternoon's games. He was a small man, with a top-heavy body and very short legs. He had a large, round head with filmy eyes that ran ever so slightly. He dabbed his white handkerchief about them as he thought once again of the easy take life had become. The saloon gave him his living, the students from the various Cambridge colleges flocking in for the beer and an occasional sandwich. But the gambling action would make him a rich man. Three or four more good years, and with the money he had already stashed away, he and Rita could head for Florida – Miami Beach and the good life. That is if Rita could keep herself in shape till then. She was developing an ass like a Japanese soldier, but then again he could always dump her for one of those young Collins Avenue beach sexpots if she didn't turn herself around. Let her stay here in fuckin' freezing Boston and eat herself to death.

There was a loud knock on the door. "Come in," Ferdie said.

Kevin, his barkeep, cracked open the door and peered into the room. "Ferdie, there's a guy here wants to pay off the Kelly kid's debt."

"Give me two minutes to clear this shit and then tell him to come in," Ferdie said. Great, he thought, another $5,000 for the bank, a step closer to Florida.

After first knocking, a tall, well-dressed young man appeared in the doorway. He wore a navy blue suit with a white shirt and striped red and blue tie. "Mr. Gallipoli?" he inquired.

"That's right," Ferdie said from behind the desk. "Who are you?"

"Jack Kelly, Mr. Gallipoli. I'm Jerry's brother."

"Sit down over here, Jack Kelly. You go to Harvard, too?" he asked, pointing to the wooden chair in front of his desk.

"No, Mr. Gallipoli. I'm not a student. I'm here strictly to square Jerry's debt with you if I may."

Ferdie grinned broadly. "You sure as shit may, Kelly. You got the money he owes?"

"Of course," Jack said turning the wooden chair in front of the desk ever so slightly so that he could see the door as well.

Ferdie noted the movie star looks of the pleasant young man before him, particularly the clear blue eyes that seemed to fix on him. "Well, where is it?" Ferdie asked anxiously.

"Mr. Gallipoli, could I first as you a question? Was it necessary to cut my brother?" Jack asked calmly.

"Hey, I'm sorry for that, truly sorry. But the kid owed a few hundred, and with the vig, the mark was growing by the day with no payments coming in. He wouldn't produce any dough. I had to show him we meant business. Sorry again. But it worked, didn't it? You're here," Ferdie laughed.

Jack laughed as well. "Yeah, I'm here, Mr. Gallipoli. Tell me, how much do you think would square the debt?"

Ferdie stared across at him. Was this guy stupid? "He should have told you — $5,000, and it's due today. I hope that's what you have."

139

"No, Mr. Gallipoli, you misunderstand my question," Jack said as he stood. "How much do you think you owe my brother for the physical harm and emotional stress you've caused him? $10,000? $20,000? What would be the correct amount?"

Ferdie stared at him incredulously. "Are you fuckin' crazy, you Irish asshole?"

Jack pulled the .38 from behind his belt, leveling it at Gallipoli and, in a quick motion, gained the angle on both Gallipoli and the door simultaneously. Moving behind the desk, he pressed the gun against the left side of Gallipoli's head. "I need you to remain very quiet and I need to see some green very quickly, Mr. Gallipoli." Ferdie's hands shook as he slowly opened the drawer, revealing wads of dollars wrapped in elastics. A number of small money bags lay on the floor behind the desk.

"You haven't been to the bank yet, Ferdie, huh? Too bad. How much is there?" Jack asked, pressing the .38 hard against Gallipoli's head.

Ferdie stammered, "There's about $10,000 here."

"Put it all in one of those bags," Jack directed.

Ferdie scooped the money packets into the bag, working frantically, his eyes straight ahead, focusing on the task at hand. "Listen carefully, my limp-peckered friend," Jack said, "while I tell you a little story. You know when my brother Tom was about three he couldn't understand why he was being disciplined by our parents. If our mother slapped his ass, he would try to slap her back and he would say 'You hit me; I hit you.' Well, Ferdie, he wasn't far wrong. His actions sum up my philosophy of life – you hit me, I hit you. The $10,000 makes us almost even."

Ferdie flinched, terrified. "Almost even? You're stealing my fucking money, and we're not even?"

Jack reached into the left pocket of his suit coat. "You weren't listening, Ferdie." With a quick motion he raised the sling blade and slashed Ferdie below his left eye down to his mouth. Ferdie shrieked in agony, lifting his hand instinctively to the area. "You cut me, I cut you, you prick. Now we're even. You ever come near my brother or me again, and I'll kill you, your wife Rita, your fuckin' father, and the whore you've been

141

seeing on the side. Do you understand me, Ferdie?"

Sobbing, Ferdie nodded.

Jack picked up the bag and moved to the door. As he closed the door behind him and headed for the exit, Kevin asked from the bar, "What's all the noise about?"

"Ferdie cut himself shaving," Jack tossed over his shoulder.

When he was back in Lynn, he phoned Jerry at his dormitory. "Hi, Jerry. Everything going okay?"

"Jack, I'm glad you called. It's Saturday. What about Ferdie Gallipoli and the money?"

"That's why I called, Jerry. I met with him, and everything is fine. Would you believe he canceled the debt?" Jack said.

"He what?" Jerry practically shouted.

"We had a good talk. You keep away from him and his place, and he leaves you alone. No more betting with any books, Jerry. Do you and I have an agreement?"

"Jack, of course. I don't know how to thank you."

"Just learn from this. You want to gamble, bet with friends and bet small."

"You and he got along and settled all this?" Jerry asked. "That's hard to believe."

"Sure we did. He's a real cut-up," Jack replied.

LYNN ENGLISH VS. LYNN CLASSICAL

"The Greatest Game" – November 28, 1946

Whatever the sport, with every heated rivalry strong debate always occurs when dedicated fans gather to discuss storied histories. Over the decades true fans reflect and genuflect when reminiscing about the Army-Navy, Harvard-Yale, Red Sox—Yankees, Duke—North Carolina series, among so many others one could mention. Memories flood back, sometimes causing distortions and revisionist history, and just as often tempers flare as the series, particular games, and individual performances are reviewed.

It is no less so at the high school level whether one is considering bitter football rivalries in Texas or Pennsylvania, basketball clashes in New York City or Philadelphia, or baseball contests in the Los Angeles – San Diego area.

Right here in Massachusetts we add to the mix by setting our greatest football rivalries on Thanksgiving Day, the series in many instances spanning more than one hundred years as neighboring cities battle for bragging rights. Today, in 2004, interest has waned a bit but, nevertheless, when Malden faces Medford, when Bourne challenges Wareham, when North Quincy battles Quincy, there is palpable excitement in the fall air.

For a variety of reasons which I will delineate, I believe there is no stronger high school rivalry than that between Lynn English and Lynn Classical, and no greater game, in that scintillating series than the 34th rendition on November 28, 1946. And I was there.

Just as societal factors have lessened interest today, they contributed strongly to the aura surrounding the game in 1946. In that particular year 100,000 Lynn residents faced a future brimming with hope and promise. Just months before, in August 1945, the second great World War had ended and weary veterans were streaming home to claim a slice of the good life, raise their children – the baby boomers – and settle into what would hopefully be quiet, conservative, sedentary lives.

Lynn provided both a comparison and a contrast to other urban centers of the time. Like most industrial cities, it was and is home to great numbers of European immigrants. Unlike them, and despite the city's unity during the war years, it was a city divided into two broad sectors, East and West Lynn. Running through the center of the city, Washington Street, in effect, separates the two. With strict policy being adhered to in 1946, those students who lived east of Washington attended English and those west, Classical High.

Encompassing a huge swath of the city from the Lynnfield line to the beaches themselves, East Lynn was a curious amalgamation of largely middle class Yankee, Irish, Italian, French Catholics and Protestants, with both a wealthy Jewish population, close to the beaches and a fairly large low income Black neighborhood near English High. I lived on Fayette Street, that street itself mirroring the sector. The lower end contained the Black population, the middle the Irish-Italian-Yankee neighborhood where I grew up, and the upper end the Jewish neighborhoods.

In contrast, West Lynn ran from both the Saugus and Revere lines to the city center. Its largely middle-class blue-collar neighborhoods were comprised of great numbers of Greek, Polish, and Albanian immigrants coupled with a solid mix of Irish and others of European extraction. Strong, vibrant neighborhoods, like its Brickyard section, brought people together in a great tide of community pride.

Although Washington Street divided the city, students from English would still attend church, say at St. George's Greek Orthodox Church in West Lynn, with students from Classical, and East Lynners worked side by side with West Lynners at the massive General Electric plant, or at Champion Light, or at any one of the huge number of downtown shops. But always there existed the division and, therefore, the bitter rivalry of separate but close neighborhoods, and various ethnic groups — their pride in both religious and national background reinforced by both school and church.

In September 1946 the average Lynner thought mainly of becoming more prosperous. Wages averaged less than $3,000, enough certainly to afford a pound of grapes at Blood's huge food market in the city center for $.19 or a one-pound cabbage for $.04. Down the street T.W. Rogers department store was offering dresses for sale from $10.45 to $16.95, and its next door rival, Burrows and Sanborn, advertised wool winter coats for $24.00.

As schools opened that September, the city was greatly interested in their Lynn Red Sox, a minor league affiliate of the Boston Red Sox. The Lynn Sox played their home games at Fraser Field, and in early September they were involved in a hotly contested race with the Nashua Dodgers, a Brooklyn farm team. The hated Dodgers were led by two Black ballplayers vying with Montreal star Jackie Robinson to become the Major Leagues' first Black ballplayer. By September 4, a Wednesday, pitcher Don Newcombe had compiled a 14-4 record and his batterymate, Roy Campanella, was hitting .301.

Down on Union Street the Warner was featuring Cary Grant as Cole Porter in "Night and Day," the latest Van Johnson flick "Easy to Wed" was playing the Paramount, while the Capitol offered the western "Renegades" coupled with the latest Blondie – "Blondie's Lucky Day" and a Hugh "Woo Woo" Herbert featurette. Over in West Lynn the alluring

Gene Tierney starred in "Leave Her to Heaven" at the Uptown.

Throughout September, Republican Robert F. Bradford battled Maurice Tobin for the governor's seat, a race that culminated in November with Bradford's election, as he became the Commonwealth's first Republican winner in years. Lynn contributed heavily to his election, the city caught up in the ultra-conservatism sweeping the nation at the end of the war. The G.O.P. also gained control of both houses that same year. (Should I write to Mitt Romney and let him know there were once grander days?)

As I entered my last year – grade 8 – at St. Joseph's Institute that September, the city's hard-working adults were seeking relaxation and entertainment largely at the cinema. (More people attended the movies in the 1940's than during any other decade in our history before or after.) They were also preparing for what seemed to be an interesting football season. With no television and with prices reasonable at $0.90, $0.60, $0.35, or $0.25, families flocked to Manning Bowl, a magnificent oval structure with 20,000 seats, built by the then mayor J. Edward Manning, with federal funds in 1936. In 1946, over 300,000 fans would attend the weekly high school games at the Bowl.

Over in West Lynn, optimism ran supreme. A veteran team led by its outstanding coach, Bill Joyce, was returning. The only concern lay with the quarterback position. Don Miosky, a fine performer, had graduated after leading Classical to an 8-3 season the previous year. He was to be replaced by a junior named Harry Agganis.

"Can Harry Agganis handle the tricky new T formation like Miosky had?" screamed the headline in the Lynn Daily Item, on Wednesday, September 4th, two days before the annual football jamboree, a series of scrimmages among area teams that would kick-off the season before 20,000 North Shore enthusiasts.

In 1946, most teams still utilized the single-wing formation, one dependent on power blocking and a running game. Across town at English, Carl Palumbo, a prime advocate of that offense, readied his first team, and, like Classical, was without a veteran tailback to trigger the offense.

John A. Curry

Post-World War II high school teams were designated in A, B, or C classifications dependent on enrollments. As examples, both Lynn schools were placed in Class A, Saugus and Marblehead in B, Winthrop in C. Following the jamboree, where both Lynn teams performed well, Classical opened the season with a resounding 39-0 victory over Class C Winthrop. That was the start of an exciting season: 12-0 over Arlington, 38-14 over Revere, 44-0 over Lowell, 27-0 over Gloucester, 26-7 over a great Salem team, all on the way to a 11-0 season.

Across town English started more slowly, losing a close decision to Salem 15-13 on a last-second field goal, and then to Beverly and Lawrence as well, before they began pounding the opposition, rolling to six wins.

The East Lynners were led by an outstanding baseball player, shortstop Charlie Ruddock, whose father did so much to bring Little League baseball and a subsequent state championship to Lynn in the early 50's. A gifted all-around athlete, Ruddock was playing football for the first time as a senior.

In West Lynn, Harry Agganis, a fine running back as a sophomore, had answered all questions regarding his abilities very early in his junior year, leading Classical to those eleven straight victories. Raised down on Waterhill Street, just off the corner from Barry Park and Jack Arslanian's cobbler shop, Agganis had shown great ability in all sports from a very early age.

Born on April 20, 1929, at age 14 he had played under the name "Ted Casey" for the Lynn Frasers, a semi-professional baseball team, batting .342 against major league pitchers such as Walt Masterson in a league that also included catchers Yogi Berra and Jim Hegan, the latter also an East Lynn native and future Cleveland backstop. By age seventeen, Agganis was generally regarded as the best high school baseball player in the state and was named as New England's sole representative to the Esquire All-American baseball game. But in the fall he was also demonstrating his prowess as a left-handed passer and a deft runner, leading the Green Wave to those eleven wins, answering all skeptics, bringing crowds of 20,000 plus to home games, gaining a reputation as the best quarterback in Massachusetts. Wearing number 33 in honor of his idol, Slingin' Sammy Baugh, Agganis was a scrambler in an era of dropback passers. His spirals were tight and precise, his running simply superb. Remember now. This was the era when the participants played both offense and defense. To document his abilities, Agganis, a safety, led the Rams in both tackles and interceptions.

On October 31, 1946, writing in the Item, Ed Cahill, the sports editor, reported that undefeated Classical would soon be invited to a national championship game in either Miami or New Orleans to face Granby High of Norfolk, Virginia, generally conceded to be the number one high school team in America.

In East Lynn, despite the late season surge, the Bulldogs virtually limped into the Turkey Day showdown. Their star tailback, Ruddock, had suffered a head concussion in the penultimate game – a win over Somerville – and junior tailback, Billy Whalen, son of the beloved principal of English, had been injured in the same contest. In addition, fullback Nick Ricciardelli was just returning from a bout with pneumonia.

Entering the clash, Lynn Classical sported that undefeated record, having scored 299 points against 40. While upping their slate to 6-3-1, the Red and Gray had scored 209 and allowed 76 points.

—

On November 28, a cold fall welcomed a beautiful day; one punctuated, though, by high winds, a factor that would figure heavily in the game to follow.

At 8:00 a.m., along with a welter of young fans, I watched the McGinn of Lynn bus leave Memorial Park, a.k.a., the Meadow, carrying the English team to Chestnut Street and then over Lynn's Highlands to Manning Bowl. We ran after the slow-moving bus as it meandered the one-mile run up to the Bowl. As the Red and Gray rode in abject silence refusing to acknowledge our cries or the applause of our parents walking to the game, the Classical team moved through West Lynn in that very same silence, totally dedicated to the task at hand – a chance at the national championship.

Ahead of the buses the magnificent Bowl filled rapidly to capacity, 20,000 seats occupied long before the 10:15 a.m. kick-off. Most men wore shirts, ties, and suit coats, and most women gaily flaunted the colors of the two schools. Outside the Bowl vendors hawked peanuts at 10 cents a bag, candy bars two for 15 cents and ice-cold Coke bottles for a dime. At each entrance to the Bowl (Classical fans naturally approached the oval from the west and English enthusiasts from the east), ushers stood ready to assist patrons to their seats.

On the south side of the field legions of Green Wave fans clustered around the ram Ophelia and slapped their hands enthusiastically as Captain Dick Crombie led his undefeated team onto the turf. On the north side, red and gray clad cheerleaders led a bulldog on a leash as the crowd overlapped into each end zone, standing three deep. In the west end zone the dance pavilion was completely overwhelmed by fans. Packed tightly against the fence separating the end zone from the pavilion, they threatened to break down the barrier itself. At the main entrance to the Bowl on Maple Street, hundreds of fans stood on the steep concrete decline leading to the field and peered into the stadium itself. Along the sidelines huge stacks of hay lay invitingly for players who would soon be tackled out of bounds.

When legendary referee Henry Hormel (he of Army-Navy fame) called Crombie and English co-captains Vin Di Grande and Marty Smith forward for the toss of the coin, the Bowl literally erupted. Crowd estimates ranged from 21,000 to 23,000.

—

The starting line-ups, again with almost everyone playing both offense and defense:

<u>Lynn</u> <u>English</u>	<u>Lynn Classical</u>
LE Jack Hennessey	Vic Pujo
LT Mike Kavanaugh	Bob Anderson
LG Bob McIntosh	Ray McClorey
C Joe Penney	Chippy Chipouras
RG Bill Driscoll	Dick Crombie
RT Vin Di Grande	Harold Potter; Fred Smith
RE Marty Smith	Nils Strom

Q	Dick Nardella	Harry Agganis
LH	Charlie Ruddock	George Pike
RH	Dick Cahill; Les Locke	George Bullard; Dick Dooley
F	Nick Ricciardelli	Dave Warden

Following the kick-off to Classical, the Rams received the message that on this day English would be playing its best game of the season. In the opening series, Agganis could not move his team, forcing a poor punt fielded by English on the Classical 35. In quick order a revitalized Charlie Ruddock turned his own right end and scampered thirty yards for the touchdown. Ricciardelli ran in the extra point.

Score: English 7, Classical 0

Later in the quarter Harold Potter blocked a Billy Whalen punt (later Whalen would kick one 70 yards with the wind), and with the ball on the Bulldog 41, Agganis displayed his magic, hitting Dick Dooley for a 26-yard completion and scoring the first touchdown himself. Dooley kicked the extra point.

Score: English 7, Classical 7

Most in the stands now awaited the onslaught of the Classical juggernaut; however, English continued to surprise the crowd, countering with an 80-yard march, featuring Billy Whalen's 41-yard rush and another of 31 by Ruddock. Ricciardelli scored on a goal line plunge and converted as well.

Score: English 14, Classical 7

The second quarter was dominated by Agganis and his running mate George Pike. During the season Pike had led all Essex County backs with 15 touchdowns, and in this, his final game, he was all over the field. A 50-yard drive culminated in a Pike score, but Dooley missed what would later become a most important extra point.

Halftime Score: English 14, Classical 13

In the third quarter a Classical fumble was recovered by Vin Di Grande, an all-scholastic on virtually everyone's list at season's end. A Ruddock to Jack Hennessey pass to the Rams' 4 was followed by Ricciardelli's burst into the end zone, and his one-point conversation rush placed Classical in dire straits.

Score: English 21, Classical 13

But Agganis moved his team following another tremendous punt by Whalen from his end zone to mid-field. Corralling the football, Agganis returned it to the English 24, and then Pike raced to the 14, and two plays later ran it in for the score. Faking the placement this time, Agganis, the holder, stood up and rushed around his left end for the extra point.

Score: English 21, Classical 20

Early in the final quarter, lanky Jack Hennessey, playing a superlative game, intercepted an errant Agganis to Bullard pass on his own 40. Passes from Ricciardelli to Hennessey and Ruddock to Whalen moved the ball to the Classical 7 from where Ricciardelli ran for his third score of the game. Vin Di Grande's kick just barely missed the right upright, causing the officials to check carefully with one anther before finalizing the call.

Score: English 27, Classical 20

With only eight minutes to play, Agganis rallied the West Lynners, throwing deep to the very speedy George Bullard, first from the 50 to the English 30 and then to the 9. Scoring his third touchdown of the morning, George Pike ran around right end for six points.

Trailing now 27-26, Agganis set the placement for Dooley, but with Hennessey and English's other outstanding end, Marty Smith, rushing to block it, Agganis quickly stood and fired a strike to Vic Pujo.

Score: English 27, Classical 27

Each team had one more chance to move the ball, to no avail. The most exciting Turkey Day clash between the bitter rivals ended in a 27-27 tie. To English supporters, a great moral victory had been earned. And Classical fans screamed in appreciation of a gallant comeback and the preservation of their undefeated season.

Outside the Bowl, young and old fans ringed the English bus, cheering the team for its effort as the boys boarded the bus. Just a few yards away this scene was repeated as the Rams climbed the steps to their bus. I shall forever remember racing between the two busses, angling to catch a look at the players.

Curiously, the boys all looked as solemn as they had on the ride up to the Bowl. No one was celebrating, players on both teams were silent, spent, depressed, hanging their heads. I remember not understanding why, and years later coming to understanding.

On Friday, November 29, the Lynn Item carried the headline, "Classical Post-Season Tilt in Doubt." On that same day more than 5,000 people watched the film of the fierce encounter at the Paramount Theater.

Over the decades there have been, of course, many other outstanding English-Classical contests worthy of our consideration as the "greatest game". But neither before 1946 nor after did we ever experience the confluence of factors that occurred that particular year:

1) Our Johnnys had come marching home victoriously from a world war.

2) Consumer confidence was at an all-time high with the city hugely optimistic.

3) People were looking forward to unprecedented prosperity following the Great Depression and the war.

4) Eager consumers had money to spend for movies and sports, with few other distractions.

5) Television was on the horizon, but had not yet influenced us to become couch potatoes.

6) A population comprised of the descendents of competitive immigrants lived in adjacent neighborhoods.

7) Strict boundary lines and school attendance policies pitted neighbor against neighbor.

8) A new coach at English faced a legendary coach at Classical with each favoring entirely different offensive systems.

9) Two strong teams, one of which went on to win the mythical national championship, faced one another.

10) Participants in the game are still thought of among the elite of Lynn's athletic heroes: Agganis, Bullard, Ruddock, Whalen, Pujo, Strom, Hennessey, DiGrande, Pike, Smith, Chipouras, and Ricciardelli. Most of them went on to distinguished collegiate careers, and some to professional ball.

Some Footnotes:

1. Classical was invited to the Orange Bowl in Miami, Florida, on Christmas night, 1946. They faced Granby High of Norfolk, Virginia, for the mythical national championship. Classical won, 21-14.

2. On Friday, the <u>Lynn Daily Item</u> praised the line play of Classical's Dick Crombie and English's Marty Smith. Following the game, Smith was sent straight to the hospital with the flu and constant nosebleeds. The <u>Item</u> declared "Smith was in on every play for the Bulldogs."

3. George Bullard, then only a junior, not only performed admirably for Classical in this game, but went on to a spectacular senior season and a pro contract with the baseball Detroit Tigers where he reached triple-A Buffalo at a time when there were only eight American League teams.

4. Charlie Ruddock, another great shortstop, was signed to a baseball contract by the Philadelphia Phillies.

5. Harry Agganis, arguably Lynn's most outstanding athlete ever, aptly labeled "The Golden Greek", became an all-American quarterback at Boston University. Incredibly, while accumulating a long string of offensive records, Agganis punted for a 46.5 average in 1949 and intercepted 15 passes in 1949 as a defensive back; 27 in his career there.

   "The Golden Greek" chose baseball as a career. Signed by the Red Sox in 1953, he became their starting first baseman in 1954 and was batting .313 in 1955 when he was stricken with pneumonia on June 4 in Kansas City. Doctors back in Boston at Santa Maria Hospital also determined he had developed phlebitis in his leg.

   On June 27, early in the morning, Harry suffered terrific pains in his chest as a blood clot in his leg broke loose and shot into his lung.

At age 26, Harry Agganis passed to Olympus, "where the Greek gods dwell" as Bill Cunningham of <u>The Boston Herald</u> reported.

Sportscaster Murray Kramer of the <u>The Boston Globe</u> wrote: "He was the greatest football player I ever saw, and I've seen them all."

An estimated 30,000 people passed through St. George Greek Orthodox Church in Lynn and 20,000 more lined the streets to Pine Grove Cemetery. Today Agganis rests directly across the street from Manning Bowl.

TRYING TO CONNECT

Brian Hughes sat in the fading afternoon sun at the Red Rock Bistro in Swampscott, the restaurant perched at the top of the sea wall, his view unobstructed on a marvelous early fall Saturday. Below him yuppies strolled on the sand at low tide, holding hands, as dogs of all sizes, perpetually in motion, chased the sea gulls, never ever with success.

To the north, above the beach, he could see the outlines of the huge Boston buildings, the John Hancock and the Prudential Center, and the financial district itself. To his right, the long sea wall ran from Swampscott back toward Lynn. Amateur runners and disciplined walkers mingled together, squeezing in their exercise before their Saturday night fun.

"When I was a kid growing up in Lynn, this place was an ice cream stand—Doane's," Johnny Casey said, trying to sip his VO and ginger slowly in front of Brian.

They sat apart from the two noisy couples at the far end of the restaurant, just a few steps from the entrance. At the maitre d's station, a haughty young woman was having great trouble understanding why she couldn't bring her poodle into the dining area. They were practically outdoors anyway, weren't they? What was the problem?

"Will you listen to that fuckin' idiot," Brian said. "First the goddamn beasts are pissing on the beach or having a dump where people walk and now they want to come in and have a steak, too. Did you read the other day about people now bringing their mutts onto planes and into first class? Next, they'll be sitting on the pilot's laps or having a shit in the aisles."

"I'll take it you're not a dog lover," Johnny laughed. "Laura has a dog."

"How's she doing? Laura, not the dog," Brian added.

Johnny set the VO down. "I called her again today. She won't talk to me."

Brian studied his friend carefully. In just seconds the manic had faded into the depressive. It had always amazed Brian, despite his readings on the subject of mental health problems, how quickly these changes occurred in those who suffered with the malady.

"She'll come around, Johnny. It's hard for her, too, you know," he said quietly, his empathy for his friend coming through.

Johnny displayed his hangdog look. "I've fucked up my whole life, Brian. You know to me she's sort of a redemption, a new chance for me to make things right. To do something right. To make another human being's life better because I'm there." Glancing up, Johnny signaled the effeminate waiter. "You want another?"

"I'm all set, John." He decided to change the subject to try and move to a happier topic. "We pulled off the heist, Johnny. A whole day gone by, and it looks like we caught them all with their pants down."

Johnny's mood did not change perceptively. "It's only been a day, Bri. I wouldn't celebrate too soon."

"Well, by Monday we'll know more. I've got a way to find out what they know, but my gut's telling me they don't know jackshit."

Johnny frowned, the lines above his eyes coalescing. "I don't feel as good about it as you do."

Brian sighed and then bit his tongue. "What's wrong, Johnny?"

"I'm confused. I felt good about it yesterday, y' know? But today…"

"Good about what? Your involvement, right? Johnny, you did things right. You came through like a pro. Be happy!"

Johnny sat still while the waiter deposited his third VO and ginger. "Brian, I was trained at BC to live a clean life, not to sin and so weren't you, too. Then we go out and rob people. It's a moral crisis for me."

"'The hottest places in hell are reserved for those who, in times of great moral crisis, maintain their neutrality'," Brian quoted.

Johnny smiled. "Richard Pryor say that?"

"Dante."

"Bichette?"

Brian grinned at him. "No wise ass. Dante. Didn't you learn anything at BC? Move off the dime, Johnny. That's what he meant. You can't worry about decisions you've already made. We've got enough to concern us, going forward. You made the decision to get involved. Let's not track backwards."

Johnny diverted his gaze toward the elongated windows and the ocean itself. A hundred yards away, four or five young boys braced themselves for the dash from seashore to the undulating waves, undoubtedly aware that in all probability this was their last swim of the season.

"I won't stay in neutral, Brian," he finally said. "I just have my ins and outs, you know? I just don't feel 100% good about being a fuckin' robber. So shoot me."

"Now that's the best thing you've said all afternoon," Brian said, reaching across the table and pumping his hand.

"Fuck you," Johnny replied, the manic expression coming on, the eyes lighting up, the grin spreading as the old ghosts receded, assisted by both friendship and the VO.

—

Johnny Casey awoke on Sunday morning, trying to remember what had happened. After he and Brian left

175

the Red Rock, he had driven over to Eastern Avenue to Monte's and sat at the bar watching the BC game. Now, as he placed his bare feet in the slippers and stood, he remembered. Virginia Tech 48, Boston College 34. Plus 14 points. Fuckin' Michael Vick and the Hokies. Plus 14 meant his $10,000 was down the drainpipe by one point. One damn point!

He must have drowned his sorrows at the bar because he could not remember much else. How had he gotten home? He wasn't sure.

The sing-song of his slippers slapping against the linoleum kitchen floor was the only sound he heard as he headed in a slow, veering course toward his coffee maker. From Lewis Street below, he caught the sight of a young boy exiting a car, delivering the Sunday papers. Little lazy bastards, he thought. When I was a kid, we walked, and we walked with the heavy bag of papers draped from our shoulders. Now parents in Mercedes drive their little cherubs up and down the street as if they were delivering mink coats. Oh, well, he thought, it takes a family to build a village.

From the living room, the telephone rang, its volume level penetrating and overwhelming. He had deliberately set it high for fear that he might miss an important phone call while in one of his frequent fogs. He let it ring a second time, trying to determine who might be calling him at nine o'clock on a Sunday morning. Ayala looking for his $10,000? He didn't need that call right now. Maybe it was Brian, but he very seldom called.

On the third ring, he quickened his pace toward the bedroom and picked the phone up. "Hello," he muttered.

"Johnny, this is Donna. How are you?"

Surprised, he almost dropped the phone, but then composed himself. "Hey, Donna."

"You all right, Johnny?" she asked, a trace of annoyance in his ex-wife's voice.

"Donna, I'm fine. Really. You just surprised me, y' know? It being Sunday morning."

"Well, the reason I'm calling is I wondered what you had planned for today."

"Planned?" he repeated, wondering where this was leading. "Not much, probably watch the Pats on TV."

"You sure you're okay? Not drinking or anything?"

"Donna, for Christ's sake. What do I have to do? Pass a physical?"

Donna paused for a moment. "Laura wants to see you, Johnny. For the last day or two she's asked me if you could take her to the movies over in Danvers at Liberty Tree Mall."

What had it been? At least a year since he had last seen his daughter? He didn't know how to react, and so he reacted poorly. "I don't know, Donna," he hesitated. "She wants to see me?" he asked, the surprise now creeping into his voice.

"Yes, Johnny. Isn't that a good sign?"

"Do you have any idea why she changed her mind?"

Donna skipped another beat before answering him. "She's almost thirteen years old, Johnny, and confused. She's hurt and hateful one minute, and happy and loving the next. She's a kid."

"Well, I thank you, Donna. I'm sure you…"

"It's her choice, Johnny. You treat her right, and make sure she has a good time."

Why was it that she appeared to be lecturing him one minute and then could be understanding and sympathetic the next?

"What time does she want to go?"

"The movie starts at 3:20 P.M."

"I'll be there at quarter of."

"Have her back here by 6:30, okay?"

"Fine, Donna, and thanks."

—

"So what are we going to see, princess?" he asked as they drove along Route 128 into Danvers, the honky tonk of the Liberty Tree Mall appearing out of the flatlands to their left.

"I'm not your princess," Laura replied coldly, her eyes riveted on the curving ribbon of highway, her concentration intact.

"Your being a princess is in the eye of the beholder. To me, you're a princess," he answered, almost defiantly, emphasizing each word.

"Well I'm not," she countered angrily.

"Okay," he sighed. "So let's get back to square one. What do you want to see, Laura? Is that better?"

Apparently not. She did not respond.

Johnny Casey tried to remember his child development lessons while pushing into the background the child psychology his father and the nuns had practiced on him. Talk sassy to an adult and a backhander would straighten out your recalcitrant ways, as defined by them, not by the child.

"I want to see 'The Perfect Storm', she announced out of the blue, as if any other option were not to be considered.

He decided to demonstrate his intellectual side. "I read Junger's book," he said.

"Who?"

"Junger."

"Who's he?"

"The author Sebastian Junger. The movie is based on his book."

"I think the movie came first, and he copied it," she declared firmly.

"Whatever, princess. I could be mistaken."

"Don't call me that name," she said, wrapping herself into herself, squishing almost into a fetal position.

He decided to retreat and play catcher to her pitcher.

They walked through the entrance to the movie complex after he paid enough money for a luncheon at Pier 4 for tickets to the movie. "Want some popcorn?" he asked.

"No."

"Your tickets are to theater #2," a pock-faced young adolescent who just barely qualified as an usher-customer services representative indicated. "It'll be available in a few minutes."

Johnny Casey scanned the indoor marquee, noting that at least twenty different movies were playing, some on three different screens.

"I think we're straight ahead on the left," he said.

They entered a graham-cracker box of a theater with maybe ninety seats, eighty of them within five rows of the screen. Instantly, he recalled the movie theaters of his youth, massive cinema palaces with thousands of seats, with the option of near screen, mid, or rear orchestra, and balcony seating. To enjoy this movie, he would have to visit the Pearle Vision Center over in Saugus first. Stop bitching, he urged himself.

In the second row , he tried to concentrate on the plight of the six swordfishermen caught in the storm of the century. Thank God he had not had any VO, or else the endless streams of water crisscrossing the screen would have capsized his stomach as well as the boat. He glanced at Laura, who seemed lost with the crew at sea, her admiring gaze concentrated on George Clooney and Mark Wahlberg.

When it ended, and lights flooded the near empty theater, he decided to initiate conversation once again.

"You like that, Laura?"

"It was okay," she said, her glance diverted here and there, everywhere, but never on him.

"Well, they were heroic men, weren't they?"

"They were dummies, Dad. Real dopes. Going out to the Flemish Cap when a major storm was coming down. They weren't heroic at all; they were just six dummies."

Talking to pre-teens was such fun, he thought, as they headed back to Lynn. She sat silently, adrift somewhere in space, for the balance of the ride. When they arrived home, she virtually jumped out of the car without a word. He watched her bound up to the front door, seemingly oblivious to his feelings, to his desire to connect. What was that old GE slogan? Progress is our most important product? You couldn't prove it by him.

FOR SERVICES RENDERED

When she died for the final time, he still felt depressed. Tom Clayton caught himself. For a moment he felt like that guy – Danny Aiello – in the movie "Moonstruck". You know, the one with Cher, where Aiello couldn't marry her because his old Italian mom was all the time dying.

Rosalie had been very much like Aiello's mom. Since age forty, she had repeatedly forewarned her only son that she wouldn't be with him much longer. She claimed to have developed consumption, or whatever it was Camille had died of. Her dying had been going on for better than forty years, through many imaginary sicknesses.

But no one could say he wasn't a dutiful son. For the last fifty years Tom had devoted himself to Rosalie, had even lost his own Cher in the process. But he had always been there for Rosalie, knowing she was a hypochondriac, but still doting on her every wish just the same.

And not easy to do with him being a school teacher, having to put up with the little bastards that call themselves students these days, the majority of them ill-mannered, contemptuous of authority, coming to school with skin showing, looking tanned in frozen Boston, having spent most of the winter radiating themselves.

After school he would go home to Rosalie, she complaining about the guy in the next apartment playing his television too loud, her own Zenith blaring like the D-Day invasion. Or he would go down to Walgreen's for her pills, the line there practically out to Huntington Avenue, while they all waited for each buyer to sign credit slips for purchases of $2.49. He spent so much time there that he practically owned stock in the company.

Then he would cook their dinner, trying hard to prepare things she might like, but seldom being able to satisfy her. As he stirred the gravy, she would sit there in the kitchen chair, the blanket wrapped around her frame, looking like Mother Teresa, except for the tongue. "Christ, can't you stir the pot and put more seasoning in?" she would say, her own cooking never much to rave about if you asked him.

For the last six years he had considered placing her in a nursing home, the one over in Revere on the North Shore. But each time he moved to act, pangs of guilt overwhelmed him. Once or twice he had even mentioned it to Rosalie. Might as well have asked her to go do time on Riker's Island. "You would send your poor mother to live alone in a nursing home? Is that what you said, Tom, if I can believe my ears? Me? Me who took care of you when you had the croup, who nursed you, who gave you life? Your own mother to be sent from her home?"

One time, he had taken her for a drive over to North Revere, showing her the nursing home from the road. "See, Ma, it's a nice place," he had said. "There's people your age to talk to, there's good staff..."

"Yeah, half of them illegal immigrants ready to pounce on my jewelry," she had replied before suddenly gasping for air.

"You all right, Ma?" he had asked.

"I'll be all right when you take me away from here," she had muttered in a suddenly whispery voice. Raising a shaky finger, she pointed across the street.

"Look over there! A god damn quarry right there. Might as well put me in the gas chamber with all that dust eating up the air."

During the last two years her choices became limited. He brought in the nursing service or rather three nursing services, the first two not able to take the abuse, the third barely holding on before he found her a place in a small nursing home at the bottom of Mission Hill, just a stone's throw from the apartment, making it easy for him to visit and also to get away whenever she became too obnoxious or uncommunicative.

Only six months ago he had taken early retirement, at age 58, tired of the daily routine over in West Roxbury. Besides visiting Rosalie each day, he walked the Hub, always by himself, the time long past when he would take up female companionship, Rosalie having stomped out that desire years ago.

And then she finally passed. After battling imaginary cancer cells, undiagnosed heart disease, consumption which could appear at a moment's notice, she simply died of old age in her sleep. But just prior to going, she still insisted that she had contacted Aids from some guy that had breathed on her.

—

The day after she died, Tom visited the funeral parlor up on Mission Hill, the one with the ornate gate surrounding its front and sides and a huge parking lot in the rear.

"I'd like you to handle the funeral arrangements," he said to the slick, polished guy in a banker gray suit and shirt. Joel Purloiner looked ironed and pressed and fitted. He hid behind dark glasses in a darkened room. His desk separated them.

"We would be honored," said Slick.

"Could you outline the possible expenses for me?" Tom asked, thinking all the time on his limited pension and his mother's $1,000 life insurance policy.

"Of course, Mr. Clayton. So much, you understand, depends on the services you would require."

Tom nodded slowly. "Right now I'm a bit down, you know? I…"

Purloiner nodded sympathetically. "That is only natural, sir. We will handle the details for you. May I ask where your mother's body is now?"

"Just down Mission Hill at Casey's Nursing Home."

"Ah. We will escort her body here and prepare it for visitation hours tomorrow." He didn't stop for a beat. Might as well have been reading from prepared text, Tom thought.

"What time would you like for visiting hours?"

"Isn't one day rather standard? Say 4-8 p.m?" Tom reached into his suit pocket. "I've prepared information regarding her obituary. I know pretty much what she would want said about herself." Actually Rosalie had prepared most of it herself. Still the boss from the grave, Tom mused.

"Yes," Slick replied, accepting the equivalent of a magazine article.

"I'll go speak to Father Carlson at Mission Church," Tom said. "I'll ask him to conduct Mass the day after tomorrow."

"Was your mother a communicant there?" Purloiner asked, smiling sweetly, looking like Peter Sellers in "Dr. Strangelove" with the loopy grin and the dark glasses.

"Not in recent years," Tom replied.

"We could speak to Father for you," the director replied evenly. "He's known to us. of course. We could save your time."

Tom nodded agreeably. "I would appreciate that."

"Could you write down some personal things about her, Mr. Clayton. That would help Father immeasurably."

"I think you'll see that all bases have been covered in the material I gave you," Tom replied.

"We will need to select a coffin," Purloiner was now saying. "I can show you some samples," he added.

"I'd like that."

Reaching into the top drawer, the director placed a brochure on the top of an otherwise uncluttered metallic desk. He then stood so that both he and Tom could view the colored publication. "We have all sorts of possibilities," he said effusively.

"Could I see some of them? I mean, are they here?"

The director provided a coast-to-coast smile. "No. I contract with a firm over on Boylston Street. The brochure will provide us with details though. Could I ask about the price range you might be considering?"

Tom shrugged his shoulders. "Moderate," he said.

"Very good. An excellent choice."

Tom thought about the comment for a moment. So far he hadn't made any choice, and something told him that whatever he ultimately chose would have been an excellent choice.

The director flipped the pages. "Ah, here we are," he announced, pointing to two pages where a variety of wood and metallic caskets were displayed.

Tom scanned the pages. "There are no listed prices," he finally said.

Purloiner smiled. "It would be a faux pas to do so, Mr. Clayton. In general, our moderately – priced coffins range from $2,000-$4,000."

"I like this one," Tom replied, pointing to a silver metallic model.

"Very good sir. I'll have it here later today. He paused for a beat. "Is there anything else with which we can help?"

Tom shook his head slowly. "I don't think so. I'm still not focusing well to tell you the truth. Is there anything else we should be discussing?"

Purloiner looked to his fingers for the answer. "Let me see," he said, ticking off the items on his fingers, acting as if this were the only time he had done a similar thing. "Flowers, the coffin, the service itself. Oh, yes, her clothes. You'll want to bring by a favorite dress or suit. And what else? H'm. I think we're ready to proceed, sir. Oh, yes, one other matter. How will you be paying for our services, Mr. Clayton?"

Talk about tacky, Tom thought. No details concerning the charges, but how will he be paying. "By American Express credit card if that is acceptable," he said.

"Perfectly." Purloiner stood as he responded. He extended his hand. "Then we will see you tomorrow afternoon. If you wish, come earlier, about a half-hour before visiting hours, and you will be able to spend time alone with your mother as well as familiarize yourself with the surroundings."

"I'll do that," Tom said.

—

Standing before her bier, he drifted back to a long ago past, back to the evergreen days when he and his friends had run through the magical Irish neighborhood over on Mission Street, when his mother was young and uncomplaining, when they needed each other so much after his father had died of the heart attack. Now she lay before him in that blue flowered dress she favored, quiet now, not demanding anything.

Funny. He didn't feel particularly sad. He really didn't feel anything. Just numbness. He tried to cry but could not. Maybe later, but he sensed he might not for a time. At eighty-four she had lived a full life. Sometimes it was time to go. Like that president of Boston University, the one who had run for governor, had said, "When you're ripe, you're ripe." But then again he had lost the election.

And although Rosalie had been difficult, he had loved her. He focused on her long, thin hands, the rosary beads wrapped about them, thinking of the future. What would he do now? Maybe travel a bit, something he hadn't been able to do in recent years, maybe he could even meet someone. It was never too late.

He was so absorbed in his thoughts that he didn't notice Purloiner till he was alongside.

"She looks peaceful at rest," the director said solemnly, probably for the fifteenth time this week, Tom thought.

"Yes."

Purloiner coughed. "You know, Mr. Clayton, in this business there is never a good moment or a good way to bring up the subject of expenses. But while we're together now, let me provide you with this material which lists the particulars."

Tom glanced at the envelope and placed it inside his suit picket. Purloiner didn't say anything else. He simply studied the casket for a few moments and then began circling the room slowly, ostensibly measuring things—the flower arrangements, the wooden portable chairs arranged in rows, the sign-in sheet at the edge of the room, the cork bulletin board featuring pictures of Rosalie before her cranky years, her eyes then luminous, her skin glowing.

Tom looked to his wrist watch when he first heard the stir of activity, the murmur of inquisitive voices permeating the outer hallways. He positioned himself at the side of the bier, her only living relative.

During the three hours he guesstimated that perhaps seventy people arrived to pay their respects, most of them neighbors from long ago or faculty friends of his. He dutifully received their condolences, reminisced with a number of them, and gradually eased into the routine, pleased to see, especially, the few elderly who remembered Rosalie from her salad days.

It wasn't until the crowd had largely dissipated that he broke away from the bier and entered the adjoining sitting room. Alone now, he felt the crinkle of paper as he sat. The envelope.

He pulled it from his pocket and opened to a single quality sheet of 8 X 11 dimensions bordered by lovely pictures of red roses. In the center were fifteen or so lines with price quotes at the end of each. He directed his attention to the bottom line — $11,340. He nearly lost his lunch as his eye wandered from the total to each item.

Suddenly Purloiner appeared in the doorway. Probably because he had a video camera hidden somewhere in the room, Tom considered.

"Everything seems satisfactory, sir?" Purloiner asked in his wimpy voice.

For whatever the reason, Tom wasn't going to let it go by. Later, he would wonder why he reacted as he did. Was he more upset by his mother's death than he had initially thought? Was the latent anger he had felt for her in recent years bubbling to the surface? Had his own personality changed by his having spent too much time with Rosalie? Probably all of the above, he would later surmise. He stood and walked to the window facing the parking lot and peered out at the few stranglers leaving now.

"I have some questions about the bill," he finally said, still looking outside.

"Is there a problem?"

Tom turned toward the director. "Yes. The problem is I'm getting screwed."

Purloiner gained a full inch. "I don't understand," he said.

Tom pointed to the list. "Five hundred dollars to transport her body from the nursing home to here?"

"Our normal charge," Purloiner replied, regaining some of his composure.

"We're talking about a distance of four hundred yards, Mr. Purloiner. You and I could have carried her here from that distance. And $200 to fix her hair? I take her to the hairdresser once a week for twenty bucks. Why the mark-up?"

This time Purloiner didn't reply.

Tom could feel his blood pressure rising. "And $2,000 to utilize the home here for four hours?"

"We must factor in the cost of our attendants," Purloiner replied defensively.

"You mean all those guys standing all around the front hall smiling at us?"

"All funeral homes wish to accommodate the needs, the wishes of our guests."

"Well I suggest in the future you might become a little less accommodating. Maybe you could then save some poor old lady with only a $1,000 life insurance policy like my mother a buck. Maybe then they wouldn't have to go to the grave in debt."

Purloiner tried a different strategy. "Mr. Clayton, I know this is a most difficult time for you ..."

Tom cut him off. "Yes, you do. And you predators take full advantage of that fact." He glanced at the list again. "I thought we agreed on a moderately priced coffin. And I'm also paying to transport the coffin here?"

"I explained we have a contract..."

"Screw your contract, Mr. Purloiner. You guys are running a racket in this country, taking advantage of people's sorrow, sticking it to us. $11,000 to bury a poor old woman on social security? What you guys ought to do is reevaluate your practices."

Purloiner stiffened. "Mr. Clayton, our business practices are in direct line with those recommended by the American…"

"It's bullshit!" Tom exclaimed, his voice rising now.

"Mr. Clayton, I do not find your language acceptable. In the future we ask that you find another…"

"Another bandit?" Tom interrupted. "I'm sure you're all fleecing the public similarly. Maybe we should bury people in orange crates?"

"If you prefer, sir," Purloiner said, turning, moving to the door.

"I think I do," Tom replied.

THE MOVIES OF MY YOUTH

By 1946, when I was twelve years old, 90 million Americans were attending the cinema every week, a figure never ever approached in the decades which followed.

The late 30's and early 40's were a wonderful time to be young and in love with the movies. In between the box-office triumph of the definitive blockbuster "Gone with the Wind" and the birth of television, we witnessed the transformation of cinema. Furthered by great technical advances such as the development of more sensitive finely grained film, improved sound recording, shadowy new lighting, the Hollywood Dream Factory produced great entertainment for both adults and children.

But it was the stars that drew me to Lynn's fleet of theatres—to the Paramount, the Warner, the Capitol, the Olympia, the Auditorium, the Waldorf, the Uptown. The movies of my youth and their stars greatly shaped my values and taught me and my friends about the way to lead life.

I hope you enjoy the memories.

SATURDAY AFTERNOON AT THE CINEMA

In the late 30's and early 40's I often journeyed to the Auditorium Theater on Andrew Street in Lynn to watch weekly serials, twelve or fifteen episode segments which clearly proved the old axiom that actions speak louder than words.

Three studios – Universal, Republic, and Columbia – produced them, and early in the 40's Republic, the acknowledged king of the serials, predicted that they would outlast any other movie type. The fact that they didn't does not take away from their influence on those of those attending movies in that time period.

Each serial was essentially cast from the same mold. Every one of the more than two hundred produced in those years contained a myriad of fights, chases, close-calls, and assorted thrills. Truly superb stunt men blended with the studios' special-effects teams to produce wonderful visuals. Along with the fights, chases, and thrills were added strong musical scores that kept your blood racing and added value to the accompanying visuals.

I had my favorites, some of which I still own on video. Each week I would anticipate the next episode of one of the following during the golden age of the serials: "Dick Tracy's G Men" (1939), "King of the Royal Mounted" (1940), "Adventures of Captain Marvel" (1940), "The Perils of Nyoka" (1942), "Spy Smasher" (1942), "The Masked Marvel" (1943), "Haunted Harbor" (1944), "Manhunt of Mystery Island" (1944), and "Zorro's Black Whip" (1944) — all made by Republic Pictures.

From Columbia I loved "Terry and the Pirates" (1940), "Captain Midnight" (1941), "Brenda Starr, Reporter" (1945), and "The Phantom" (1943).

And Universal provided "Buck Rogers" (1939), "The Green Hornet" (1940), "Don Winslow of the Navy" (1942), "The Adventures of Smilin' Jack" (1943), and "Sky Raiders" (1941).

The actors were a stock company of heroes and villains, 90% names you would not recognize then or today. I think I favored the villains, particularly Roy Barcroft who played Captain Mephisto in "Manhunt of Mystery Island" or Charles Middleton as Ming the Merciless in "Flash Gordon" (1940). Among the heroes I loved Ralph Byrd as "Dick Tracy", Tom Tyler as "Captain Marvel" and that same actor as "The Phantom," Don "Red" Barry as "Red Ryder," and Tom Brown as "Smilin' Jack". Curiously, not many of the actors and actresses who appeared in the serials went on to stardom, but there were a few exceptions. Ruth Roman appeared in "Jungle Queen" in 1945, Frances Gifford in "Jungle Girl" (1942), and Bruce Bennett, then called Herman Boix, in "The New Adventures of Tarzan." (1941). Did you know Joan Crawford's husband in "Mildred Pierce" was a former Tarzan?

Each episode or chapter of a serial would last for twenty to twenty-five minutes, 90% of them in fifteen installments, the balance in twelve. Inevitably, each segment would end with our hero or heroine in a precarious state, being thrown off a cliff, tossed into alligator waters, falling from on high into a flaming wagon, along with many other life-threatening situations.

My friends and I would wait all week for the next installment, as we all do today for Tony Soprano. If we missed an episode for good reason, we could always find someone among us who could tell us how Buster Crabbe had escaped Ming's clutches in Chapter 8.

As I grew into my teen years, we witnessed the death throes of pulp fiction and radio shows such as Jack Armstrong and Captain Midnight, and unfortunately, we also observed the serial fade into obscurity. After better than forty years of continuous entertainment, inquisitive youths would turn to other directions rather than watch larger-than-life heroes overcome the apostles of evil.

Television, of course, really hurt the serials. You could now watch a complete action series like "The Cisco Kid," "Hopalong Cassidy," "Sky King," etc., right at home. In addition, movie studio serials became too expensive to produce, and they never really provided great revenues anyway. At their zenith, in the early 40's, they provided a few dollars in rent back to the studios who used them as an incentive to force the theater to take their other studio productions.

And something else happened post-World War II that hurt the serials. I loved them because the good guys always wore white. The heroes were all good, and the villains all bad. No ambiguity at all. But in the mid-forties mothers and fathers came to believe the Saturday cliff-hangers were filling our young minds with violence and assorted mayhem. In addition, psychologists advocated that pure villains like Captain Mephisto might really have been the victim of a deprived childhood. Say what? Republic threw in the towel in 1955, but long before that the serials had died.

For those of us still yearning for youthful escapism, the birth of video saved the day. Now my grandchildren can sit with me and watch Captain Marvel overcome the mysterious Scorpion, Spy Smasher gain the advantage over the evil Nazis, and Kay Alredge as Nyoka defeat the evil Vultura.

Who says black and white isn't better than ambiguous gray?

JOHN GARFIELD

I have always been infatuated with the gritty urban dramas produced by the Warner Brothers. As the famed New York Times critic Bosley Crowther said in reviewing Cagney's "City for Conquest", my favorite childhood film, "Sometimes we wonder whether it wasn't really the Warners who got New York from the Indians, so diligently and devoted have they been in feeling the great city's pulse, picturing its myriad facets, and recording with deep compassion the passing life of its seething population."

No studio did New York stories better than the Warners. They captured the essence of its people, the crowds who intoned pure New Yorkese, and they produced a stable of stars – Cagney, Bogart, Robinson – who were born and bred in the Big Apple and, who, therefore, always seemed so natural.

One of my 40's favorites was John Garfield, the original rebel without a cause. He was a street kid, raised in the Bronx and on Manhattan's lower east side. He represented the collective fantasies of city kids such as I, the sons and grandsons of urban immigrants residing in America, seeking the American dream.

In his early deterministic films (1935-1943) the cynical wise guy, searching for that dream, often makes strong-headed moral decisions until someone, usually a woman, rights him. Garfield was almost always a type, his characters barely shifted from film to film. Although he clearly lacked the range of some of the other Warners' stars, he came to represent an image, that of every city youth who dreamed of wealth, of escaping the ghetto.

And, of course, he was based at the right studio, because the Warners were the social documentarians of America. A Warners film was always different in looks and feel from those of MGM or Paramount or Fox. They described, particularly in that stretch of my coming of age, the problems we faced every day – poverty, crime, the mysteries and injustices of society, all done in a less glossy way compared to the other studios.

Ultimately, soon after his early death at age 39 in 1951, Garfield's persona was adopted by the 50's rebels – James Dean, Marlon Brando, to name just two. Cocky, alienated suspicious, frequently playing a drifter in his early films, Garfield was our 40's anti-hero.

In "Body and Soul" (1947) Garfield as crooked boxer Charlie Davis shows us an arrogance that conceals his vulnerability as well as his despair as he wrestles with demons, unable to speak about his inner fears. He is the ultimate outsider, lashing out at all the suckers.

He frightened me in "Out of the Fog" (1941) as a small-time shakedown artist beating up on Thomas Mitchell and John Qualen. And in that same year he was paired with Edward G. Robinson and Ida Lupino in Jack London's "The Sea Wolf". Although his part was clearly secondary to Robinson's in this depiction of fascism run rampant, his scenes with Ida Lupino create sexual energy not often seen in the era of the production code.

I loved him in 1943's "The Fallen Sparrow," in which he plays a former prisoner-of-war in Franco's Spain who returns to New York to unravel his friend's death. He displays the perfect edginess of a man haunted by nightmares of his torture when captive. A trained stage actor, he easily conveys inner turmoil and mental anguish. I can still see the perspiration falling from his face as he hallucinates about his captors and the fact they may now be in New York. I don't believe I've ever again seen such a harrowing depiction of a man trying to maintain his mental stability.

In 1946 he was loaned out to MGM to appear with Lana Turner in "The Postman Always Rings Twice", a pairing made in heaven. Based on James M. Cain's novel of adultery and murder "Postman" contrasts the rugged darkness of Garfield with the blond glitter of Turner, all dressed in white when we first see her – white shorts, a white halter and a white turban.

In those Hayes production code days, sex was implied, not displayed, and in "Postman" the chemistry, the subdued sexuality between the stars was just enough. Year later, in the re-make with Jack Nicholson and Jessica Lange the sex was flagrant, on full display, but still proved the old adage that most of us look better with our clothes on.

Although Garfield left us too early, his success as an actor – both on Broadway and in Hollywood – served as an affirmation for the millions of urban Americans who fought against the great depression and the social structures holding down "the little guy".

JUDY GARLAND

I grew up on Judy Garland. When she began winning over radio audiences in 1935, I was just a toddler, but I grew into puberty as the MGM star worked from 1935-1950 for the most glamorous of the Hollywood studios.

She was my idealized girl next door – clean, decent, self-depreciating, witty and especially accessible. No one of MGM's "more stars than there are in heaven" could connect with an audience the way she could. When she sang with that full-throated voice, there was something desperate and physical in there, the conveyance of real melancholy and sadness. She sang of loneliness in a way never better expressed before or after.

What do I really know about music? Not a great deal. But she touched me with music that had heart. And I always felt that one of the greatest singers on earth was singing for me alone. If it is true that true art comes from pain, then her art ran in rivulets – through her soul.

Like nearly all young children, I was taken off to see the Wizard in 1939, but I didn't really fall in love until 1942 when she came of age in "For Me and My Gal," paired with Gene Kelly in his very first film. The movie itself was a salute to vaudeville and takes place during World War I but, of course, in 1942 with America at war, the story was topical. She and Kelly made a wonderful team, dancing and singing their way through the title song and through a great rendition of "Balling the Jack". It is also here that Garland introduced "After You've Gone", displaying her ability to mimic Sophie Tucker cadences in a song she used throughout her later career as a concert singer.

In this film she was no longer the adolescent, but instead, a young woman in love, with the need to express that feeling. This was a new, more adult Garland graduating from a type of female Mickey Rooney into a star showing signs of acting talent, as she played a singer in love with a draft dodger (Kelly).

I was in the sixth grade at St. Joseph's Institute in 1944 when "Meet Me in St. Louis" came to Lynn in the winter of that year. It played at the Paramount, where all the MGM films were shown. In the 1940's no other studio could make musicals with the panache of MGM, and "Meet Me in St. Louis" displayed Garland at her best singing "The Trolley Song", "Have Yourself a Merry Little Christmas" and "The Boy Next Door". Only a curmudgeon would object to the film's serene pastel-hued fantasy of home life. Remember, in 1944 most of us had both a mother and a father living under the same roof.

In 1948, she made "Easter Parade," another one of my all-time favorites, with the great Fred Astaire. Although kind of a standard show-business story, the film contained seventeen Irving Berlin songs, including the title song, "When that Midnight Choo-Choo Leaves for Alabam'", "A Fella with an Umbrella," "Happy Easter", "It Only Happens When I Dance with You", and the marvelous "A Couple of Swells" where Garland and Fred dressed and romped as tramps. Years later, when she left MGM and conducted concerts, she would almost always incorporate the "Tramp" into her act.

John A. Curry

In retrospect, she conveyed a purity that we all wanted in all girls of the 40's, and her 40's pictures frequently carried the message that there's no place like home, whether that home was Oz, Kansas, St. Louis, or Broadway. She once said that "the history of my life is in my songs" and indeed it was. The heart-rendering voice could capture the essence of unrequited love which we all faced as teens in songs such as "Dear Mr. Gable" and the sad Gershwin tune "But Not for Me". During my coming of age, I was always happy the greatest female vocalist of all time was singing just for me.

JAMES CAGNEY

For us post-Depression kids, James Cagney is remembered as the All-American king of the gangsters, as the personification of the relentless man of the streets, fast of foot, good with his fists, and extremely dangerous with a gat. We were shocked at the way he handled women in films like "Public Enemy" (1932). He could be sweet and gentle, but if his women got out of line they got whacked. Our perfect hood even surprised us by proving himself a song-and-dance man in movies such as "Yankee Doodle Dandy" (1943) for which he won the Academy Award.

Along with Bette Davis, he was the biggest of the Warners' large stable of stars. Another New Yorker (Do you get the impression all of my favorites are from Gotham?), he appeared as the common man. Like so many of us, he worked hard to combat the social structures seemingly set against him. He exuded confidence and a kinetic sort of energy in overcoming adversaries, or he poked fun at ridiculous establishment figures that made rules meant to be broken.

In the late 30's and early 40's, he was often paired with another New York City actor, Humphrey Bogart. In those days Cagney was the more established actor as it was not until a string of successes – "High Sierra" (1941), "The Maltese Falcon" (1941) and "Casablanca" (1943) – that Bogart elevated himself from a "B" to a major actor.

In that same period, Cagney not only won the Academy Award, but thrilled us by a number of superior performances, as a belligerent dentist in "The Strawberry Blonde" (1942), as a cowardly soldier in "The Fighting 69th" (1940), and as a blinded boxer in "City for Conquest" (1940).

I can remember seeing "City for Conquest" at the old Waldorf Theater in Lynn and being mesmerized by the Warners' depiction of the aspirations of an East Side boxer and his dancer girl friend, the lovely Ann Sheridan, each of them trying to break loose from poverty and move out of the tenements. I have never seen an actor portray a blind person as beautifully as Cagney does in this film. He cocks his head to catch shadow on the periphery of his limited vision; he walks with a cane in measured, irregular patterns across a room. He draws our complete sympathy toward a man injured in an unfair fight. "City for Conquest" is my favorite Cagney film because of its evocation of the importance of aspiration, of our overcoming adversity.

Common to virtually all of Cagney's films was an emphasis on the importance of character. He was always confident, frequently to the point of brashness, and he made errors and hurt people as many of us do in our developmental years, but ultimately he redeemed himself as we were taught to do in those war years by our parents, our religious leaders, and our schools.

When he left Warners to form his own independent film company in 1943, the quality of his films suffered. Movies like "Johnny Come Lately" (1943) and "The Time of Your Life" (1948) were too arty for a young boy.

He came back to us in 1949 in "White Heat", back to the front ranks of gangsterism. He played Cody Jarrett, a murderer subject to epileptic fits and a mother fixation. He reeks of vigor and is eloquently sardonic.

We kids saw him again as in happier days, a bit jowlier, heavier also in voice, yet pummeling society with a tigerish grin on his face.

Cagney represented the perfect urban boy and man at a time in our lives when the Depression and war made us insecure. Years later mimics would imitate his walk, his steadily mounting rage, his use of his entire body to convey virtually every emotion. He exuded a cocky conceit and an impish charm. His range was extraordinary – war films, gangster films, comedy, musicals, westerns, spy stories.

He was an original, unabashedly American star whose 30's films were replayed consistently throughout the early 40's at the Waldorf in particular. I couldn't wait to see his next movie or one of his old ones, as he was always giving us clues as to the proper living of an urban life.

ALICE FAYE

In 2000 I wrote a crime novel entitled "Two and Out". Its plot concerned the coming together of four different characters to pull off two separate robberies before leaving the life. One of the perpetrators – a man I called Vic Fleming – is a retired, dishonest cop with a fixation on the movie star Alice Faye. In reality, I transferred my own obsession to Vic Fleming.

In 1939, just as my interest in the cinema was beginning, Alice Faye's star was as bright with movie audiences as the stars in heaven. Under contract to Twentieth Century Fox, the soft, natural hair falling about her shoulders, her large expressive eyes, and that warm, incredible voice had all become trademarks of the most popular star of that time.

I went to Lynn's Paramount Theater early in 1939 to see her in "Alexander's Ragtime Band" and immediately became enthralled with Irving Berlin's songs and the artist singing them. The movie contained almost thirty songs from Berlin including "Blue Skies" "A Pretty Girl is Like a Melody", "Heat Wave", "Easter

Parade", "Oh! How I Hate to Get Up in the Morning", "What'll I Do?" and the rousing title song.

Paired with Tyrone Power and big-voiced Ethel Merman, Faye projected a quality of resolve. In her films she was almost always "the good girl," one who suffered almost silently because of some man – usually Tyrone Power, John Payne, or Don Ameche. When she cried, you cried. And she told of her mistreatment through her songs, songs of elusive love and heartbreak.

She looked like Jean Harlow but with warmth under the sheen that Harlow lacked. She could sing, and she could act, displaying wide emotion as she sold a song. Her picture on the cover of sheet music sold more copies than that of any picture star of the times. She was not a great beauty, what with her forehead being a bit too high, the nose upturned, the cheeks a little too prominent and full. But her eyes were something else. Vividly blue, they expressed the sincerity of the star. Topped off by long, velvety lashes, the Faye eyes could not be resisted by many.

In her movies, she would sing hugely popular songs standing virtually still beside a piano or against a pillar. The voice was smooth and natural as she sang Academy Award winners like "You'll Never Know" in 1944's "Hello, Frisco, Hello". There was something wistfully plaintive in Faye's voice that tugged at the heart. Her singing was quiet, and extremely effective in all her films.

During the period 1939-1945, I raced to see films such as "Rose of Washington Square" (1939), "Tin Pan Alley" (1940), "Lillian Russell" (1940), "Hello, Frisco, Hello" (1943), and "Fallen Angel" (1945).

Like MGM, Fox studios loved to produce musicals. But there was one big difference between the two. The MGM musicals such as "Seven Brides for Seven Brothers", "The Pirate", "Meet Me in St. Louis" were made with settings gigantic in proportion and very original. In contrast, Fox's settings in the Faye musicals or Betty Grable's were very static; normally the cameraman would just shoot straight from the audience onto a stage.

Without that all-seeing eye, the target had better be good. A natural, Alice Faye would let the mouth tremble ever so slightly, look to the camera with those expressive eyes, bend her right leg at the knee, and draw you to her song. In an era where musical story lines were very similar (boy meets girl; misunderstanding occurs; boy mistreats girl; girl forgives), Alice Faye was the screen's foremost popular singing artist. In 1940, the Showman's Trade Review named her the nation's outstanding female box-office draw, ahead of Bette Davis, Olivia DeHaviland, and Myrna Loy.

I still visualize her dressed in a blue evening gown decorated with sequins, leaning against a table, propping a telephone against her ear, singing my favorite love song "You'll Never Know". The voice deep and throaty, full of love and sensitivity, Alice Faye made you want to hug and comfort her. You believed in her and wanted the girl next door to be just like her.

JOHN WAYNE

It is a fact that most Hollywood personalities achieve stardom only gradually. In my youth, in the days of the "studio system," most of the stars-to-be served long apprenticeships in minor roles. For example, Bogart served as a "B" star in a long series of potboilers until he broke through in Raoul Walsh's "High Sierra" in 1941.

In the late 30's John Wayne had already made 63 films before his star-making role as the Ringo Kid in John Ford's epic western "Stagecoach" (1939). Although we youngsters had seen him any number of times in "B" westerns and Saturday afternoon serials at the Auditorium Theater over on Andrew Street, we didn't really separate him from other cowboys until "Stagecoach". His initial work was almost all accomplished for small studios such as Monogram or Republic, and prior to 1939 he averaged six films a year. In some of those films he worked with other future stars, such as Alan Ladd, Marsha Hunt, and the vivacious Phyllis Isley (later Jennifer Jones).

I can still picture the exact moment when he became my hero. In "Stagecoach" he is standing in the middle of a dusty trail, a saddle in one hand, a Winchester in the other, firing rounds in the air to halt the oncoming stagecoach. If I remember, his horse had gone lame. The sequence – introducing Wayne for the first time in the film – lives in memory because of the camera work, which starts in the long distance and zones in on the cowboy standing there.

Remember in the early 40's we wanted heroes, clear-cut ones, not ambiguous psyches. The good guys wore white, and the bad guys black with little room for grey in the middle. We loved our cowboys because they mirrored our everyday lives. Right was right, and wrong was wrong, just as we were taught at school. The bad guy always got his come-uppance. There were no anti-heroes.

In 1942 Wayne made two films with Marlene Dietrich and Randolph Scott – "The Spoilers" and "Pittsburgh". In that same year we went to the Auditorium to see him fight for the Chinese government in "Flying Tigers". Upon leaving the theater, I immediately cast my younger brother Marty as the evil Scott or as a Japanese pilot and pummeled him in the alley next to Anthony's Hawthorne Restaurant, or in the huge post office on Willow Street where he ran to escape, or inside the cemetery on Union Street where he tried to hide. Later, he became too big for me to chase down.

Also in 1942 the Paramount featured our hero in Cecil B. DeMille's lavish Technicolor spectacle "Reap the Wild Wind", a story about shipwrecks on the Florida Keys. I can still see Wayne in his deep sea diving suit warding off an octopus in order to save Ray Milland (a pansy to us kids). I saw the movie eleven times.

In the early 40's Wayne alternated between cowboy and war leader roles in films such as "The Fighting Seabees", "Back to Bataan", "They Were Expendable", "Dakota" and "Flame of the Barbary Coast". We flocked to see him get the better of villains like Albert Dekker, Mike Mazurki, and Ward Bond, as he made us proud to be Americans. In those days when heroes were both respected and revered, John Wayne provided stability and conscience to America's young. We idolized and yearned to emulate the man in the white hat's manner.

He wasn't a great actor, but later, in his very best films, he showed far greater range. For example, in 1956's "The Searchers", in my opinion the greatest western ever made, through both speech and manner he gave as good a portrayal of a racist as I have ever seen.

In the early 40's we never wondered, "Where have you gone, Joe DiMaggio?" because we had our heroes and chief among them was John Wayne. After all, if we didn't have Wayne, I wouldn't have had reason to pummel my brother, the villain.

BARBARA STANWYCK

Of all the screen actresses of the late 30's and early 40's, I enjoyed watching a tough lady from Brooklyn the most. Barbara Stanwyck could play everything from soaps to horse operas, high to low drama, comedies to potboilers, musicals to westerns. I loved her because of her durability and the fact that she possessed such great range. She could be con artist, prostitute, reporter, stripper, gun moll, lover, society girl, rancher, gambler, mother, and daughter. You name it; she could play it.

What all of her women characters had in common were toughness, a strong determination and self-assurance, and a quick wit. She had that well-modulated alto voice, with tones that deepened as the years went by. She would speak virtually through clenched teeth with exemplary posture, making you believe that you were observing a real person, not just an actress.

During the period 1939-1945, I saw almost all of her pictures. I still possess the video of one of my favorite westerns – Cecil B. DeMille's robust "Union Pacific" (1939), where she played a tough Irish post mistress in a rousing film that introduced Robert Preston to the movies. In that same year she made us believe she was a frank and cynical Jerseyite in William Holden's first film – "Golden Boy".

In 1941 the great director, Preston Sturges, presented her as a con artist in "The Lady Eve". Here she displays a flair for high comedy and shows us how a woman can be beautiful, sexy, romantic, and devious all at the same time. And in that same year I saw "Meet John Doe" where Stanwyck pairs with Gary Cooper in Frank Capra's fine film. They mix so beautifully together – the shy, bewildered Cooper so upset with world conditions and the tough but brittle Stanwyck suddenly finding herself in love.

I enjoyed Stanwyck movies largely because of their witty dialogue. In two of my favorites the writing was done by the gifted Billy Wilder, who later became one of our great directors. In "Ball of Fire" (1941) Wilder spoofs the academic community and kicks around our language in this lark of a comedy concerned with slang. Prissy professor Cooper learns from yum-yum Stanwyck as Sugarpuss O'Shea, a worldly temptress who teaches him about slang, and, more importantly, about life. I can still picture her dancing to Gene Krupa's "Drum Boogie".

In "Double Indemnity" (1944) Wilder teamed with Raymond Chandler and wrote and directed for Stanwyck the role for which she is most remembered – the predatory Phyllis Dietrickson, she of the suggestive remark and the ankle bracelet, which draw a smitten Fred MacMurray into a murder plot. She is destructively lurid and amoral as they deliver the lines which still ring true fifty years later.

"I wonder if I know what you mean," says Stanwyck, leading MacMurray into their affair.

"I wonder if you wonder," he replies.

I saw "Lady of Burlesque" in 1943 at the Warner. In this murder mystery, Stanwyck played Dixie Daisy, a stripper fending off the advances of a comic (Michael O'Shea) while they both pursue a killer of the strippers.

In "Sorry, Wrong Number" (1948), she played a bed-ridden neurotic in a movie based on the old "Suspense" radio show. A woman hears two men, on crossed telephone wires, plotting the contract murder of a woman later that night. In a grand-de-force performance, alone much of the time on the screen, Stanwyck takes us through varying stages of the woman's mind as she gradually comes to understand she is the intended victim. She passes from irritation with the phone company, to annoyance, to worry, to terror as the movie progresses.

Tough and sentimental, vicious and vulnerable, glamorous and sexy, Barbara Stanwyck created a virtual gallery of characters that still linger in the memory. I loved her pictures because you almost invariably were exposed to a new side of her through each film.

TYRONE POWER

As young boys we were all about adventure. When I was six, in the second grade, my father presented me with a Gene Autry gun and holster set, one of three presents (not 100) I received for Christmas, 1940. I remember chasing my brother Marty around our tenement apartment or having him peek around corners while I stood on a chair, hanging a picture, ready to be shot in the back by "that dirty little coward that shot Mr. Howard."

Actually, Mr. Howard was Jesse James, and my brother was supposed to be Bob Ford, the back shooter. My mother didn't really appreciate my knocking her pictures off the walls so we had to move our play outdoors, where it belonged anyway.

"Jesse James" was 20th Century Fox's big outdoor hit of 1939 and starred the dashing, handsome Tyrone Power as the doomed outlaw in a highly romanticized but splendid Technicolor film. It also starred Henry Fonda and Randolph Scott, but they were tame and lethargic next to my hero, who robbed trains, gave money to the poor, and made fools of corporate America.

Power was studio head Daryl Zanuck's favorite star, and certainly one of mine in those years. He was urbane, intriguing, a swashbuckler to be emulated. In the early 40's he appeared in a string of movies that were spectacular to a young boy. With sword in hand, he proved the equal of Douglas Fairbanks, Sr. and Errol Flynn in subduing the villainous Basil Rathbone in "The Mask of Zorro" (1940). After seeing the movie, I built myself a wooden sword, the better to cut up my brother to the chagrin of my mother. That same year, Power was named "King of the Box Office" along with Bette Davis.

I don't think I have ever seen a color film any more beautiful than "Blood and Sand" (1941), which won the Academy Award that year for best color photography. See it sometime on video, and let me know if you ever before or ever again have seen such brilliant hues on film. Power is a swaggering matador who takes up with a mistress (Rita Hayworth) while cheating on his wife, Linda Darnell (then only seventeen).

Next I saw him in "A Yank in the RAF" (1941) with Betty Grable, just about the time World War II was beginning. In this pro-British flag-waver, Zanuck mixed romance, comedy, and war action with exciting aerial footage of the Battle of Dunkirk. Power is cocky, appearing as we imagine an American would act under the circumstances – brave and heroic.

As young boys we were very much enthralled by what we read – stories of the South Seas, of lands far away from New England, of waters warm and a life different. In the winter of 1942, when a third grader, I sat at the Paramount in Lynn, the scene of all the 20th Century Fox's first run features, and watched a film based on Edison Marshall's adventure novel, "Benjamin Blake". Zanuck put Tyrone Power back in costume for a film he called "Son of Fury". Power was once again a stalwart hero who tried to right wrongs and overcome the enemy in the form of the terribly evil George Sanders as his dastardly uncle intent on depriving Power of his fortune. The film also introduced a breathtakingly saronged young woman to film – Gene Tierney, who just two years later would zoom to stardom as the enigmatic "Laura" (1944).

In the film Power surmounts an unfaithful lover and that unscrupulous uncle as he takes us between 19th century London and the South Sea islands. Having read Stevenson's "The Count of Monte Cristo" around this time, it was easy to become infatuated with this tale of revenge.

And I loved him in "The Black Swan," released in the fall of 1942. This film marked the height of Tyrone Power's career as a swashbuckler. It is a rousing tale of piracy on the high seas, with Power paired with the Queen of the Swashbucklers, Maureen O'Hara. In another beautiful Technicolor production, Power fought off the likes of George Sanders once again, Laird Cregar (a great character actor – "This Gun for Hire," "I Wake Up Screaming" – who died at age 27), Anthony Quinn (yet to become a major Hollywood star), and Thomas Mitchell (Gone With the Wind).

The string ended with 1943's "Crash Dive", Power's farewell performance before entering World War II. A submarine adventure, "Crash Dive" balanced

Power heroics with a triangular love affair involving Anne Baxter and Dana Andrews. As usual with a Power vehicle, "Crash Dive" blended dazzling Technicolor with great action and exciting romance. Was there ever any doubt Baxter would choose Power? There was no one on film anywhere near as handsome.

In the early 40's I would frequent the second-run theaters like the Olympia (which played the Paramount's leftovers) and the Auditorium, to catch Tyrone Power in films of the late 30's, like 1938's "Alexander's Ragtime Band," "Rose of Washington Square" (1939), where he teamed with Alice Faye in a thinly disguised account of Fanny Brice's rise to fame. Through this film the movie career of the great Al Jolson came to an end.

Later in his career, following World War II, I saw him in films like "The Razor's Edge" (1946), "Nightmare Alley" (1947), "Witness for the Prosecution" (1957). But even though his acting was sharper, more focused, more intense, he was never more my idol, my hero, than in the films of my early youth.

Tyrone Power's grave at Hollywood Memorial Park is marked by a while marble bench overlooking a beautiful pool. It is inscribed with the famed couplet from Hamlet: "Good night, sweet prince, and flights of angels sing thee to thy rest."

A screen and stage star like his famous father, Tyrone Power Sr., my hero made us test our manhood. We wanted to be like him, and besides, the girls adored him.

BETTE DAVIS

A number of movie critics believe there are two kinds of successful actors and actresses – those who by craftsmanship project an image, a flair for the camera to which the majority of fans react favorably, and those whose personality is so forceful, so strong that we adopt them. In addition, say the knowledgeable ones, a great star must display considerable range, and somehow be at one with the cultural, moral, economic, and political trends of her time.

I knew I liked Bette Davis but as a callow youth could never really understand why. My friends loved the glamour pusses — Hayworth, Turner, among others – and I hesitated to tell them I preferred the ugly duckling up there on screen.

Later, much later in my life, I grew to understand her appeal. In the late 30's and early 40's when my values were being shaped by a variety of institutions, Bette Davis was the prevailing feminist. Granted her films were not overwrought with feminist themes, she, nevertheless, conveyed a sense of the "new woman" rising up from subservience. Women loved her, wept openly at her films, as they observed one of their own confronting obviously inferior males (George Brent, Leslie Howard, and Franchot Tone) and winning, declaring a new-found independence in a time period when most women were clearly held back.

But what about men or boys like me? Men are probably fascinated by those women less cloying, women who have our interests at heart. When a woman is hard to master, the male becomes more aroused, more interested.

Bette Davis wasn't very pretty, in fact she lacked conventional starlet prettiness, but her eyes were popping, her speech clipped and staccato-like, and her walk swiveling. Her intelligence shone through as did her drive and ambition. Part of her appeal stemmed from the fact that she was different. I could never find the essence of her under the myriad layers of the many disparate characters she portrayed. She was mysterious, elusive, a challenge whereas most of her contemporaries were one-note sexpots. She made me think.

I first saw her in "Jezebel" (1938) in 1940 when it repeated its engagement at the Waldorf Theater. I was mesmerized by a film far from the usual southern tale. No sweet heroine, Bette's performance is a tour de force. She won a second Oscar portraying a selfish, willful woman who learns humility.

In 1939 I saw "Dark Victory" and worried myself sick about her, after all she has a brain tumor. In a film that could have been nothing more than emotional flimflam, Davis's tenderness, her sincerity, allow the movie to surmount sentimentality and make us concerned for her life.

My favorite Davis film is "Now, Voyager" (1942) which I saw at the Warner. In this film Davis rises above the material in the role of a neurotic daughter, unloved by a dominating mother, in a film whose music by Max Steiner still lingers in the memory today. Davis shows us repression at a time in film history when no one knew what the word meant. Her Charlotte Valle is close to insanity, an ugly spinster who is turned into a chic woman through therapy. Before our eyes she transforms herself as she also helps Paul Henreid's little girl out of depression. But Henreid is married and in some ways unavailable to Davis. As he lights two cigarettes at once, one for him and one for her, Davis goes about as far as the production code and the Hayes office would allow in those days – "Don't ask for the moon when we have the stars," she tells him as the film ends.

Of course I was only eight to eleven years old at the time, but I appreciated her versatility – as Mildred the whore in "Of Human Bondage", as a nearly unrecognizable queen in "The Private Lives of Elizabeth and Essex" (1938) (with Errol Flynn), as secretary to a curmudgeon (Monty Wooley) — in "The Man Who Came to Dinner" (1944), as a singer doing "They're Either Too Young or Too Old" for our soldiers in "Thank Your Lucky Stars" (1943), and as a vile murderess in "In This Our Life" (1942).

Besides everything else, she was an Essex County girl, from Lowell. Who couldn't like her?

THE BUS TO FOXWOODS

They stood just outside the senior center in Saugus waiting on the bus, Emma with her Armani umbrella, the one her son had given her, on her arm despite the beautiful summer day, Amanda wearing her long coat in the event winter should return again to New England this June.

The other passengers were still inside, sitting at the tables yapping with the other seniors – the ones who wouldn't be taking the trip – talking about everything and nothing.

Emma turned from the center to the driveway, peering through the sun spreading about them. "The bus is late," she said cantankerously to Amanda.

"Indeed," Amanda replied.

"We should report them to the town manager," Emma said.

"What's he care?" Amanda asked.

"Well he's the one that puts out the notices that if you don't have your leaves out just right – you know in open barrels or leaf bags – the town won't take them.

And he also says they have to be ready by 7:00 a.m. And he wants to charge trash fees, too."

Amanda nodded. "I see where you're going."

"Exactly. Then he should make the busses run on time as well, instead of thinking of ways to up our fees 'cause he can't raise taxes by law. A fee is a rose by another name."

"I'm going back in and complain to the director," Amanda said.

"Wait a bit. I see the bus coming now. Humph! Next thing you know the town will be asking us to ride our bikes to Foxwoods."

—

In the entrance of the parking lot Jamie Wilcox watched the two old ladies while his partner studied the racing form.

"Will you look at that old bat carrying an umbrella on a day like this?" Jamie asked.

Wilmer Smith stood under a sprawling oak tree, its leafs umbrellaing the lot, providing some shade from the already humid day. He was maybe 55, but looking older what with the whiskey taking its toll. He offered a serrated nose like Ted Kennedy's, a florid complexion, wide ears like Clark Gable's or rather like Elisha Cook Jr., for whom his mother had named him. Not for Cook per se, but for the wimpy gunsel he had portrayed in "The Maltese Falcon" back in 1941, you know the guy Bogart kept belting – Wilmer.

"You sure these oldies but goodies got any money?" he asked Jamie sheepishly.

Jamie shielded his eyes from the sun as he watched the bus pull up in front of the entrance. He was close to sixty, a little pale, but with intelligent eyes, dark hair and strong shoulders, just two months out of Walpole.

"They got cash, lots of it. They save up for the trip to the casino, maybe even set limitations on what they'll spend, but I figure with two busses, fifty crows on each bus, we're talkin' $20,000 easily."

He cost a quick glance toward Wilmer, who still studied the racing form. "You into this or not?"

Wilmer looked up. "What do ya mean? I'm here ain't I?"

"Physically maybe, but otherwise I'm not sure. Pay attention to what's happening here."

Wilmer studied the two busses. "They're not boardin' yet. And when they do, it'll take eight years to board what with them bringin' half of Saugus with them."

"How about the drivers? You observin' them?"

Wilmer leaned back against the tree. "Both of them look like they got knife and fork disease. They ain't gonna cause us any problem."

"Now remember I'll get on the first bus and you take the second."

"I heard you the first time."

"Well, hear me again. This may not be as easy as it looks."

"What time is it now?" Wilmer asked.

"You didn't bring your watch?"

"I forgot."

"You'd forget your ass if it wasn't wrapped around you. How you gonna synchronize the hold-up with me if you don't have a watch?"

Wilmer thought on it. "I'll ask one of the ladies for the time," he finally said.

"I like that. 'Pardon me you old bat. Could you tell me the time so's me and Jamie can rob your valuables?'"

"You worry too much."

Jamie straightened up and waited for Wilmer's eyes to focus on him. "And don't forget the cells."

Wilmer grimaced. "That I don't get. What makes you think these old people got cell phones?"

"The whole world's got cell phones today, Wilmer. The other day I visited my sister over in Peabody, the one with herpes? She's got two kids, one in the sixth grade, the other maybe five years old. The little one – she named him Prescott — with a fuckin' name like that I told her he had better know how to fight. Anyways, he's got a cell phone."

"At five?"

"Yeah, Sheila says he needs it to call his friends. The kid's even got call waiting."

"What the hell they talk about at five years old?"

"Probably those ads showing sexy little six-year-old girls put out by the department stores. Anyways, some seniors here will have cells. We don't need some grandma callin' 911 and saying 'Hello? Is this the police? We're being held up by some bad men, before we can hand our cash over to Foxwoods!' — So get the cells first: Got it?"

Wilmer nodded, thinking about it. "Someone could lie, hide it."

"Then you scare the shit out of them before they do. And then you be observant. If you see someone with one to her ear, grab it fast and smack her. Set an example for the entire bus."

"Hit a senior?" Wilmer asked, astonished.

"Yeah."

"My mother's a senior."

"Just lightly. So they're scared to move against us. See those men starting to board?"

"Yeah."

"There's only four or five of them. The lecherous bastards will be all over the women, tryin' for fast feels so they won't be payin' much attention to us. But watch them. One of them could try to be a hero."

Wilmer's mind was elsewhere. "So Nick picks us up near Foxboro, near the stadium?"

Jamie looked exasperated. "I told you that. In Norwood. We collect the dough and the jewelry, and then have the bus drivers stop, pull over to the side of the road, and there's Nick in the stolen car right behind there. He drives us back to Boston by goin' through the towns. Braintree, Norwood, y'know. We keep off major highways."

"Maybe we should hit 'em after Foxwoods, not before. They'll have their winnings," Wilmer said.

"Foxwoods will have their winnings, dummy," Jamie replied. "It's time. They're almost all on board. Let's do it."

They each reached for a duffel set on the ground aside them and proceeded to the busses.

"We're a little young for this group," Wilmer said, his eyes canvassing the area, looking for any sign of trouble.

"I cased the place last week and the week before that," Jamie replied. "People of all ages are takin' advantage of the trips they sponsor. They even have a lunch every day inside the center. Charge you a buck and a half for roast beef, half the town there eatin' off the toll, bitching at the same time about their taxes. You ready?"

"No problem."

"There better not be."

It took close to a half-hour for the seniors to board the two busses. Each driver had them form a long queue snaking its way back to the front door. In the lobby itself friends waved to the voyagers as if they were leaving for Cancun instead of the one-and-a-half hour trip to the Indian reservation.

Holding his duffel in his right hand, Jamie did not look conspicuous as he made his way to the back of the line for Bus #1. Almost every boarder held some sort of duffel bag or a Stop and Shop plastic bag, probably containing their Depends, he thought, as he searched out Wilmer, standing in line outside Bus #2, conversing with a couple of the talking machines.

He wasn't up for that. A couple of the women in his line were giving him the eye, not looking at him the way they should have been, wondering about a stranger, instead looking at him like he was beef for dinner. Jamie smiled warily at one who looked like she was primed for a direct assault.

At this time Nick should be waiting in the parking lot over at Burger King on Route One South. No question about that because Nick was 100% dependable, not like Wilmer who was more apt to marry one of the cuties than take their money. He caught himself. Maybe he was too tough on Wilmer. After all, Nick should be more dependable. He was his brother, wasn't he?

As he reached the bus, Jamie surveyed the situation. The old crows were just like students attending their first day of school. Instead of taking seats near the front of the bus, they clustered at the rear, talking a torrent, giggling. When they saw his Sig Sauer later that would shut them up, he thought.

There was one lone empty seat just opposite the driver. No one else wanted to sit there as long as there were other seats, not wanting to appear alone and lonely. For him it could not have been more ideal. From there he could both dominate the driver and gain easy command of the bus.

When every one had boarded, the driver, the guy who looked like an ad for Before Before and After instead of Before and After, yelled through a microphone in a gay voice, trying to outtalk the revelers as he described where they could and couldn't urinate. Jamie listened attentively to him, trying to gauge how much trouble the driver might be while he hoped Wilmer was doing the same.

On the second bus, Wilmer chose the exact same seat as Jamie. Across from him two of the ladies were getting into their seats, the one the other called Emma, fussing with her umbrella, maybe expecting the bus roof to spring holes. She wasn't tall enough to fit it into the bulkhead above her.

"Could I do that for you?" Wilmer asked.

"Why, aren't you nice," Emma replied.

Wilmer flashed her his coast-to-coast smile and lifted Amanda's duffel bag as well.

"Planning to hold up the place?" he teased.

"Aren't you funny!" Amanda said.

"Only kiddin,' " Wilmer said.

Emma studied him for a beat. "Are you a member of the senior center?" she finally asked.

"Not really," he replied. "I go to just a few things."

"Well, I haven't seen you much," Emma said.

"Maybe that's because I just got out of the joint," Wilmer said, a glint in his eye.

"Oh, Emma, isn't he so funny!" Amanda said, the emphasis on the "so", the way the kids talk today, the old crows learning from the kids, instead of the other way around. No wonder the country was going to the dogs, Wilmer thought.

"So what games will you be playing today?" Wilmer asked, liking the conversation, enjoying people as he always did.

"I like the slots," Emma replied.

"Twenty-one," Amanda said. "And you?"

"Blackjack, but I set a limit, y'know?"

"You do?" Emma said.

"Oh, yes. I bring no more than $200 to the casino. If I lose it, that's it. I think it's important to set limits."

"We do too!" Amanda exclaimed.

Wilmer crossed his legs, smoothing out the crease in his Joseph Abboud pants. "I'm curious," he said, trying to figure out what they had, then he could mentally multiply that number by the fifty people on the bus. "How much do you bring?"

As the bus driver pulled away, following the first vehicle, he announced they would be showing a DVD today – "The Whole Ten Yards" with Bruce Willis. Jesus, Wilmer thought, why didn't they just stick a porn flick up there if they were going to show that.

"Exactly like you," Emma was saying. "I bring $200."

"Me too!" Amanda countered.

"I'm Joe," Wilmer said, extending his hand across the aisle.

Emma's eyes lit up as she replied. "I'm Emma, and this is my friend Amanda."

"Well I am so very pleased to meet you both," Wilmer smiled. "I don't know why I did not make your acquaintance earlier at the center. Such lovely ladies as you."

Amanda gained a half-inch and Emma ran some fingers through her hair. "And what do you do at the center?" she asked.

"What do I do at the center?" he repeated, not really knowing what anyone did at the center.

"I just sit around," he finally answered.

"I bet you're eyeing the ladies," Amanda grinned.

"Amanda!" Emma exclaimed.

"We do line dancing," Amanda continued, undaunted.

"Now that's where I've seen you both before. I knew you looked familiar. Like Ann Miller and Rita Hayworth?"

"Flatterer," Emma replied, flattered.

—

As they sped over the Tobin Bridge into Boston, Jamie considered the situation. Without question Nick would be right behind them now, the slow-moving busses easy to follow. He glanced at his watch. In less than half an hour they would leave Route 128 and enter 95 South. Crossing onto 95 would signal both him and Wilmer into action. He had figured it would take fifteen to twenty minutes to ensure the cooperation of each of the drivers, scoop up everyone's cell phone and then, like the ushers in church on Sunday, pass down the aisle, duffel extended, and separate everyone from his/her money and jewelry. Then he would have Portly, the bus driver, pull over to the side, Wilmer would have his driver do the same, and then they would both move to Nick's vehicle.

Perfect. He didn't see how anything could possibly go wrong. Standing to stretch, he canvassed the assembly carefully. Only three men on board, all three of them between eighty and death it looked like, all three of them completely absorbed in the ladies.

"It's a long trip isn't it?" one of the ladies to his right, seated directly behind the driver, said.

"Yes, it is," he replied, sitting immediately, reaching for the sports page, not wanting to get into conversation with someone he might have to smack aside the head minutes from now. He glanced at his watch once again.

—

"Do you have the time, Emma?" Wilmer asked. From the corner of his eye he watched the sign for the Furnace Brook Parkway in Quincy flash by.

"It's exactly nine o'clock," Amanda volunteered.

"I hope I win," Emma said suddenly.

"Well, if you lose, you won't lose much," Wilmer said.

"Oh yes, I will," Emma smiled, her hands interlaced around her pocketbook. "I don't have much you know. It costs so much to live these days."

"Tell me about it."

"Yes, I will," Amanda said.

"Amanda, he didn't mean that literally."

Wilmer grinned at them across the aisle. "No, no. I'm interested."

Emma looked at Amanda. "You go first."

Amanda leaned forward, placing a hand on the back of the driver's seat. "My late husband left me with a pension of $600 a month and Social Security provides me with $900 a month. I own our home on Central Street, but our taxes and fees go up all the time…"

"They're even talking about a trash fee now. Next thing you know Amanda and I will be hauling the dump on our backs, like mules," Emma said.

"You interrupted me," Amanda said.

"Well I have to get a word in edgewise, dear," Emma replied, placing a hand on top of Amanda's.

Amanda smiled sweetly. "Well, tell your story."

"I have only a $400 pension and $1,000 a month from Social Security. And then those Republican talk show hosts like Rush Limbaugh have the nerve to criticize FDR. If it wasn't for him, Amanda and I would be starving to death," Emma said.

"So you each get by on around $16,000-$18,000 a year?" Wilmer said, glad the nuns back at Sacred Heart in Lynn had taught him to multiply.

"Before taxes," Emma said. "It doesn't leave much, especially with inflation."

Wilmer frowned. "Maybe you shouldn't be gambling," he offered warmly.

"We have to have some fun," Amanda said

"All I do is buy a $5.00 lottery ticket once a week, and Amanda and I go to Foxwoods once or twice a year," Emma said.

"And we play bingo," Amanda interrupted.

"Is your mother living, Joe?" Emma asked.

"In a nursing home over in Lynn," he volunteered too quickly.

"I bet you're the kind of man who visits her frequently," Amanda said.

"I do. Before she went in, she was facing the same money problems you just described. She's on Medicaid now. She doesn't have much."

With a lull in the conversation, Wilmer stared at the back of the first bus as the overhead signs indicated they were just five miles from the intersection of 128 and 95.

—

As soon as they turned onto 95, Jamie moved to action. It was important to appear more animated than he really felt, in order to freeze them into inaction.

He withdrew the Sig Sauer from his duffel and stood, his voice rising as he did. "All right, everyone. Pay attention to me, don't do anything foolish, and no one will be hurt!" he bellowed.

"What the hell is this?" the driver screamed in unison with some of the passengers.

Time for lesson #1, Jamie thought. He smashed the Sig against the driver's shoulder, drawing some more screams from the passengers.

"Keep driving or you won't ever be driving again!" he yelled, leaning into the driver's ear. "Give me your cell."

Obeying instantly, Portly handed across his mobile.

"Now everybody listen up! How many of you have cells with you? A show of hands right now!"

Maybe a dozen of them raised a hand.

"Now I'm going to pass down this aisle, and I want those of you with the cells to toss them into this duffel. Everyone, you hear? Because if I see anyone with a cell after I collect them, that person ain't goin' to Foxwoods. They're going to the graveyard. Got it? Now let's see them cells! Raise them on high!"

Turning to the driver, Jamie set the Sig against the man's temple. "You keep going on a straight line, same speed. I don't want any trouble from you, pal. You with me?"

The driver trembled, a thin veneer of perspiration showing on his upper lip. "Just tell me what you want me to do," he said.

Walking briskly down the aisle, Jamie stopped where the hands showed, remembering to snarl and to stare at some of the group with icy cold eyes. About two thirds of the way down, he was presented with another opportunity to frighten them into submission.

"Who do you think you are, sir?" demanded one of the few men on board.

"The Rock," Jamie responded, jamming the Sig into his stomach, being careful not to cause serious injury but enough to cause obedience.

"Aaah!" the man screamed.

"Shut up!" Jamie yelled. "Now every one of you get your cash into your hands, and your jewelry, too. When I reach the back of the bus, I'm coming back down this aisle and when I do, I want to see you place your goods into this duffel! Clear?"

"You're an awful man!" one grey-haired woman next to the emergency exit yelled.

"Anyone hiding anything from me will get what he got!" Jamie exclaimed.

—

Wilmer surprised himself. When the bus wheeled around the ramp leading to 95, he should have been on his feet, springing to action. Instead, he sat there, thinking too much, occasionally glancing over at Emma and Amanda, wondering how his mother was doing at the nursing home.

"And how old is your mother?" Amanda asked sweetly.

"Eighty-two."

"Why she's my age!" Emma exclaimed.

"Do you have any brothers and sisters?" Amanda asked. "You know, to help you with her?"

"There's just me," Wilmer replied, thinking on it.

"Well, she's very lucky to have a fine son like you," Emma said.

Wilmer wasn't so sure of that, but he was suddenly sure of his next step. He reached inside his sports jacket, searching for the stolen cell.

He stood and walked slowly to the rear, thinking he could make the call easier if the unisex lavatory was unoccupied. As he passed down the aisle, a number of the older women nodded at him. A sheep among wolves, he thought.

Entering the lavatory, he sat on the seat and dialed the number.

"911. Police Emergency. How may I help you?" a female dispatcher asked.

"Here's a tip. There's a robbery in progress on the bus to Foxwoods from Saugus. A Circle Line bus. A guy's rippin' off the whole bus right now. His accomplice is following in a car. Route 95 South near Canton."

"Sir, could I have your name?"

Wilmer cut the line. Standing, he moved quickly to the front of the bus.

"We missed you," Amanda said, smiling.

"Amanda! You must forgive Amanda, Joe. Sometimes she's too forward."

"You're both good company," he replied smiling.

Ahead of him the first bus slowed, ready to move to the shoulder of the road. Nick was just slightly behind the second bus now, easing himself into a position in the middle lane where he could easily pull ahead of the first bus at the designated site.

As they passed the Norwood town line, Nick accelerated and pulled onto the shoulder, three hundred yards ahead of both buses.

"Why that motorist just pulled over and stopped!" Amanda shouted. "And now the bus is stopping too."

"What the hell?" their bus driver yelled.

"I don't like swearing, young man," Emma said.

"I think the bus is stopping just to see if the motorist needs assistance," Wilmer said calmly. "We should go right by them. They're okay."

"I think you're right. No need to form a parade," the driver said, continuing straight ahead on the ribbon of road.

In the distance Wilmer could hear the first sound of sirens and from his position near the window and the passenger side mirror could see State Police vehicles racing toward the first bus and Nick's car.

The balance of the way to Foxwoods he feigned sleep, considering the situation. By this time, Jamie and Nick would be in custody, each of them eligible for a life sentence as two-time losers. No way, Jamie would suspect him, and even if he did, he wouldn't be doing much about it from Walpole.

As they pulled into the Foxwoods casino lot, Amanda turned in her seat. "My other friend's on that other bus."

Wilmer offered his arm to Emma as the bus ground to a halt at the main entrance. "I'm sure they'll be right along," he said.

As the three of them touched ground, Wilmer offered his hand. "Well, ladies, I hope you enjoy the day."

"We will. I feel lucky today," Emma said.

"Well, he careful now. There's lots of thieves about would like nothing more than to steal money from our senior citizens."

"I've got mace," Amanda said.

"You've got spirit, Amanda," Wilmer said. "You remind me of my mother. See you now."

He wandered over toward the parking lot where he could boost a car, get back over to Lynn, maybe visit his mother in the afternoon, be sure she was secure from any unsavory thieves lurking about at the nursing home.

SWEET AS SUGAR

When I become old, I remember thinking back in the 40's and 50's, I'll remember to tell the young about him. Just as, when I was young, I remember the old men telling me of Jack Dempsey, and Benny Leonard, and Harry Greb. But then again, maybe our thoughts about the greatness of others rubs off on us because we lived during their times.

I remember thinking that when I'm old and the young assault my senses with then unknown new "singers" and reject my Sinatra CD's, I'll turn the conversation to boxing and talk of Robinson because they never could have or would have seen anyone like him. They wouldn't be able to argue with me.

In the 1940's and 1950's and 1960's when he reigned supreme, people referred to him always as "Robinson", the appellation enough to stir deep respect and admiration. Sugar Ray Robinson's real name was Walker Smith, Jr., and he fought professionally from 1940 to 1965, an amazing span. Engaging in 202 pro bouts, he lost only 19. He held both the welterweight and the middleweight titles at a time when it was highly unusual for a boxer to fight at both 147 pounds and 160 pounds, long before we invented a multitude of phony divisions and titles.

Starting out as our Golden Gloves amateur featherweight champion, the sleek, rangy stallion of a kid from Detroit went on to list among his conquests this outstanding gallery of boxing greats: Henry Armstrong (a champion himself across three divisions); Jake La Motta (Robinson won 5 of 6 bouts against him including the infamous "St. Valentine's Day Massacre" in 1951), Tommy Bell, Jimmy Doyle (Doyle died of head injuries following their bout in 1947), Kid Gavilan, Rocky Graziano, Robert Villemain, Charlie Fusari (Robinson dropped back down to welterweight for this 1950 bout), Bobo Olson (four times), Randy Turpin, Carmen Basilio, and Gene Fullmer.

Sugar Ray Robinson was the man. In all of boxing lore, save perhaps for Muhammad Ali, there is no image more regal than Robinson cruising through Harlem in his pink Cadillac. No one before or after him has so magnificently combined style with substance and accomplishment.

It was a newspaper reporter named George Case from Watertown, New York, who first wrote that his boxing was 'sweeter than sugar'. As a boxer, he flashed amazingly fast feet and even faster fists thrown almost always in combination. He was both a master boxer and a terrific puncher (110 knockouts in 175 wins). He could take you out with either hand.

Because of the 1980 film "Raging Bull" people confuse the basic ease with which Robinson disposed of Jake La Motta. The one time of six that La Motta outpointed him (1943) Robinson, then a welterweight, was fighting a strong middleweight.

In the 75th year of its publication, Ring Magazine declared Sugar Ray Robinson the best fighter ever over Muhammad Ali, Joe Louis, and Henry Armstrong. In addition, his knockout of Gene Fullmer in 1957 in Chicago (at age 38) was voted the best knockout in ring history over Rocky Marciano's K.O. of Jersey Joe Walcott. He fought for the middleweight championship at age 40, called then the greatest fighter pound-for-pound ever. He was the master of masters in the period between 1940-1950, just before the era of TV boxing.

I still remember listening to Don Dunphy describe his skills on my bedside radio, pre-television.

In 1952 he even tried to move up to light-heavyweight (175 pounds). On a blistering June night at Yankee Stadium he almost succeeded, ultimately succumbing to the 104 degree heat, giving away fifteen pounds to boxer Joey Maxim. Robinson was way ahead on all three judges' cards when he collapsed in his corner at the end of the thirteenth round.

He didn't compile a perfect record, but he fought from age 15 to 45. He didn't transcend the ring and symbolize his era as Ali did, but he spanned three decades in times when champions fought frequently, facing the same strong challengers (La Motta, Turpin, Olson) any number of times.

Granted like most fighters he stayed too long at the dance, but he nevertheless fought from featherweight to light-heavyweight. Can you name any other fighter who crossed so many weight classifications from 120 to 175 pounds?

The social circumstances of his era forced him to take to the ring and to fight as many as 129 amateur bouts (never defeated) and those 202 professional fights, a total of 331 bouts. There were so many other great fighters, some even named "Sugar", such as Sugar Ray Leonard, but there is only one fighter known a) immediately by his last name b) as the greatest ever pound-for-pound, a term forever associated with him, and c) the best combination boxer who ever lived. Robinson.

INSPIRATIONAL PEOPLE

Ruth Hatch looked exactly like a female Ichabod Crane – tall, lanky, leaning forward slightly as she literally bounced around our classroom on the first floor of Lynn English High School back in 1949.

She was my own Ms. Chippings, a teacher of United States History who made the events of our country's growth come alive through her intellect, her keen analysis, and her Socratic method of teaching. She wore long dresses that didn't particularly become her, and her hair, pulled back in a tight bun, took something away from the slightly bemused smile she frequently offered. But I found myself often staring at her, waiting for new pearls of wisdom to spill forward while listening to her description of a given historical event.

Back in 1949 at English, I was exposed to wonderful teaching that helped shape my later interest in history and in our language. I remember fondly many of the teachers of English High: Mr. Thorne, a diminutive, bespectacled, brilliant teacher of Algebra and Advanced Math; Mr. Rousseau, an engaging science teacher; Miss Wildes, my sophomore English teacher, who first interested me in the classics; Miss Shepard, our gracious, literate librarian who taught me the value of books.

Of course we were not naïve, even back in that conservative day. As with today, we knew good teaching, we knew when we were being shortchanged, and that we might eventually pay a penalty for incompetence. As an example, in my sophomore year the geometry teacher graded us on the number of times we could copy a particular problem from the blackboard. In those pre-Ricoh, pre-Kinko days, we were still imaginative enough to find countless ways to gain an "A" or a "B" with no concurrent understanding of the geometry involved. I paid the price when I entered Mr. Thorne's Algebra II class the following year, not knowing a triangle from a rectangle.

Of all my teachers, I considered Ruth Hatch the very best. Years later I would understand that she was outstanding because of a number of factors:

1) Before she taught us a thing, she spent the first week or so setting the stage, outlining the rules of

procedure, her expectations of the class, the disciplinary code she would invoke, and seating arrangements.

2) Once we knew the rules, she began teaching, surprising us immediately by calling us all by our names. "What do you think about Alexander Hamilton's strategy, Mr. Curry?" she would ask, her eyes piercing and probing. Whatever I did or did not know about the strategy, I was thrilled to be called by my name, even if so very formally. She knew me, and that meant so much to a less than confident youth.

3) As she involved us, she moved about the room, always multiply conscious of everything going on around her – a singular dullard trying to catch some z's in the corner, a misfit shooting paper clips across the aisle, a romantic dreamer doodling on his paper-covered book. All were noticed and swooped up in her net: "Mr. Rogers, are we boring you? Mr. Johnson, would you be kind enough to stay after class and sweep up those paper clips? Mr. Smith, are you with us today?"

I, among many others, was with her every day.

4) Ruth Hatch taught history so that we might live history. She supported her considerable dramatic recitations of historical events through audio-visual presentations, through key map-making assignments, through challenging questions i.e. "What exactly made Teddy Roosevelt such a unique leader? Why did Southerners consider the Northerners hypocrites regarding the issue of slavery? Why was Clemenceau critical of Wilson's Fourteen Points?"

5) She was neutral. Neither a Republican nor a Democrat be, to paraphrase Hamlet's uncle. She espoused no one's agenda, except knowledge. Learn to think, she was saying to us. Accept no givens. Recognize manipulation.

6) She understood the importance of covering curriculum materials. In 1949, and for many years before and after, U.S. History courses across America began with our drive for independence from King George and ended ... where? Usually in 1890, before the Spanish-American War, or maybe just before World War I. Not so with Miss Hatch. We grew to learn of the Great War, of the rise of nationalism, and

of communism and fascism, of the reasons for World War II.

Across the hall from Miss Hatch, another teacher of U.S. History provided a strong contrast. Moving in an entirely opposite direction, she insisted on absolute adherence to principles which virtually closed the door to knowledge, i.e. read the textbook chapter by chapter, outline each chapter, underline all key phrases, assure margins were proper. Ugh!

My Ms. Chippings taught us to think, to appreciate and cherish our rich history, to value people and the importance of the loss of any one of us.

I am sure we have all known a Ruth Hatch, teachers who inspire us and challenge us, teachers who help us become better people than we were before exposure to them. When I am gone, and some stranger or other reviews my career, my hope is that someone, some former student, remembers me as I remember Ruth Hatch – as a teacher who taught, who elevated thinking, who cared enough to remember names.

One day Miss Hatch told me that "My business is to mold young men and women." She did that.

John A. Curry

At her retirement party she told us "I will never forget your faces. In my mind, you remain my boys and girls. Remember me sometimes."

I always will.

THE INTERVENTION

He swallowed rather than sipped the Crown Royal. The ads said it was to be enjoyed much more if you sipped it, but you couldn't prove it by him. For a science teacher it was really a matter of pure logic. If you drank it in swallows, the amber worked its way into your system more quickly, the heady feeling then came on faster, blotting out reality, numbing the senses – the desired result.

Chris Travis signaled the bartender for another and as she turned to fill the order, Chris studied the room. Not much of a crowd, he had to admit. At 4:30 p.m. only a few singles lined the bar at the Hardcover over in Danvers.

After school each day he drove the five miles north from Lynn, wanting both to separate himself from the city and from any prying eyes as well. He caught himself as the vivacious blonde server placed the Crown Royal on top of a paper napkin. In 2004 he should be worried about prying eyes? He remembered reading that as recently as forty years ago the behavior of public school teachers was thoroughly scrutinized.

Today you could practically bed the seventeen-year-olds with no one complaining as long as the girls took the pill. Today the inmates and their parents were running the asylum.

But still, it was no one's business if he wanted to drink alone. Besides which, he knew when to stop, didn't he? He could handle six or seven. Sometimes it was that seventh one that put him under, but only sometimes. Sometimes he just needed the seventh.

At least here, sitting alone for an hour or two, he could think straight and drink straight, not have his mother carping at him about his inbiding, she herself having downed enough bourbon in her day to float a boat. Or his best friend, giving him that holier-than-than look while he himself was settling in on his third marriage-go-round. And after a day of putting up with today's teens, he needed an end-of-day drink or three.

"Hi", she said, sliding into the stool while in the background Bette Midler was impersonating Rosemary Clooney, or trying to, the diva hard enough to take when she was doing her own shtick, the latest something called, "Kiss My Brass."

"Hi," he replied, coldly, not wanting any company, not wanting to hear of someone else's problems when he had enough of his own—the family, the job, Marlene, just to scratch the surface.

He couldn't really tell if she was coming on to him, not at first, because she busied herself with the bar menu. "I'll have a Virgin Mary," she finally said.

Why come to a bar for a Virgin Mary, Chris thought. Go visit a kid's lemonade stand along the street in any town or city.

"And some cheese and crackers, please," she added.

He hoped she didn't say another word. To ensure his privacy, he considered the drink and ever so gradually turned his body away from her. And he fingered the newspaper he always brought with him, to put off the talkers. At the moment he was trying to read about Pedro Martinez's latest ultimatum when in reality El Gripo's words were blurring.

"So what's new in the sports world?" she asked. She either wasn't a student of body language or like most of today's aggressive women didn't much concern herself with initial put-downs.

"Not much," he replied, not eyeing her, that is until he felt her staring at him.

Then he looked across at her. She was dressed in a short skirt and business jacket, a business woman seeking some respite from the daily grind. She was pretty, in a plain sort of way, her eyes fetching beyond the pale complexion. Observing her, he still decided that drink was the better companion.

"Bartender," he said, raising his hand, "the bill, please."

"I hope you're not running away on my account," the girl said, keeping her voice light, not wanting to show any hurt.

Chris examined the bill and pulled $40.00 from his wallet. "No, of course not," he replied, forcing a thin smile to his lips. "I have another date," he replied standing. "Have a good night."

As he meandered through the aisle leading to the front door, he wondered how quickly he could reach the bar at the Ninety-Nine over in Lynnfield.

—

"Thanks for stopping by, Chris."

Peter Gregory knew enough to start their conversation with amenities but despite the principal's smile Chris could guess exactly why he had been summoned.

"Did I have a choice?" Chris laughed, trying to demonstrate his sense of humor, his poise when he had actually lost both some time ago.

"We've got a problem, Chris."

Chris flinched but kept his decorum. He hated that "we've" stuff when in actuality old team player Gregory didn't think he ever personally had any problem at all.

"We do?" Chris replied, playing the game. But he knew "we" would soon change to "you".

"Your attendance, Chris. I'm concerned about it."

"I've missed a few days," Chris conceded amicably.

"More than a few, Chris. What's today? May 8," he said, looking quickly at the wall calendar. "You've missed seventeen days this school year."

"So?"

"And you've been late five other times."

Chris let out a loud sigh. "Peter, I don't know where you're going, breakin' my balls and all, but I've had a bad year, more colds than usual, y'know? Am I not entitled to be sick?"

Gregory tented his fingers onto his lips. "Of course you are, Chris. But I think your absences are symptomatic of a deeper problem."

Chris leaned forward and held the principal's stare. "Which is?"

"I think you're drinking too much."

"You think?"

"I know."

Time to act indignant, Chris thought.

"You know? I'd like to know how you know," he bellowed, as he stood. "Because frankly, I don't know what the hell you're talking about."

"What do you think the temperature is in this office, Chris?"

"What?"

"The temperature."

"How the hell do I know and who cares anyway."

"It's 60 degrees inside and outside as well, and you're sweating. And you look like shit – pale, drawn, and sweating early in the morning most mornings…"

"I've had a bad winter."

"It's May."

Chris stood and pointed an angry finger at Gregory. "You got a problem with me, Peter, take it up with the union. I get fifteen days sick leave a year and have used them. So what? Why don't you spend a little time on some serious problems around here instead of raggin' my ass. Like teachers who can't teach, like kids wanderin' around in here with shivs, like curriculum books that are outdated…"

"You're in denial, Chris," Gregory replied calmly.

"And you're full of shit!" Chris screamed, turning, storming from the office.

317

—

Marlene now only called sporadically – maybe five or six times a year. With no children to bind them together, why would a divorced spouse need to call him anyway? He couldn't really answer his own question, but even after two years, he still longed to hear her voice. When she did call it was usually concerning a tax matter, an insurance question, a lingering bill. It didn't matter to him, he always tried to prolong the conversation.

He hadn't seen her for more than a year now, but he could picture her, he could still fantasize. He envisioned her good English skin, the short nose with the bow lip, the dark black hair that he used to tease her about – "You look like a mescalero apache," he used to say in the days when they had both thought of love as something real and tangible, and everlasting, an every day happening that would never be taken away.

She had that voice which was at once tinny and tiny, and that little girl way of tittering at his silly jokes, at least in their good days. And there had been a number of good days, more than ten years of them, before ... he caught himself. Before she took off, ran out on him.

Chris Travis slammed the refrigerator door closed as a point of emphasis. He didn't feel much like eating anyway. Over at the Danversport Yacht Club there would be a spread of cheese, maybe he'd order some nachos as well.

He glanced at his watch. 5:30 p.m. He would leave for Danvers right away so he could stop thinking about Marlene running out on him. He had heard she was back to dating again. One of his friends had seen her over at Anthony's Hawthorne-by-the-Sea in Swampscott falling all over some guy popping oysters into his mouth, some old guy who looked like Kris Kristofferson with the Santa Claus beard.

He thought on the booze. It was time to go. Fuck Marlene. He was sure someone was.

—

His mother looked a little bit like a green heron – what with the big snoozola, the snake eyes, the eyebrows plucked raw and redrawn with a green pencil. Marlene had nicknamed her "The Witch" because her lips were thin, her chin pointed, like Margaret Hamilton's when Judy Garland went off to see the Wizard.

When the cell beeped, he saw it was she. Should he answer? He always felt ambivalent regarding Norma, even about answering her calls.

If he picked up, would he be greeted by Dr. Jekyll or Mr. Hyde? When she wanted to, Norma could be gay, effusive, enthusiastic, and comfortable. And when she had a hair across you-know-what, she made Mr. Hyde look like Adam Sandler.

He decided to answer.

"Yes, Ma."

"Hello, dear," she said. "I thought you weren't going to answer me," she said testily.

"Sorry, Ma. I'm at a meeting."

"Yes," she said facetiously, "I can hear the tinkle of glasses in the background."

"It's a business meeting, Ma," he responded dully.

"Where are you, dear?"

None of your God damn business, he almost replied. "I'm over at the Continental with some teachers," he replied instead.

She hesitated for a beat, probably trying to decide whether to make an issue of his drinking for the tenth time this month or to get on with whatever else prompted the call.

"I need you to give me a ride on Monday," she finally said demurely. "Can you do that for me?"

"On Monday? What time?"

"After school. In the evening in fact. I'm going to a diabetes workshop at Union Hospital. I have a ride there, but I need someone to pick me up at 7:30 and Margaret can't…"

"No problem, Ma," he interjected. If she kept on talking, his Chivas would turn watery. "I'll be there at 7:30 Monday."

"Make a note, dear. I'll be in Room 101 in the basement area. And, dear…"

"Yeah, Ma?"

"Please. No drinking. You know how scared I become when you've been drinking and then have to drive me."

Was there anything worse in this world than a reformed drinker? Maybe a reformed fat ass, he mused. When one of them lost ten pounds, they suddenly became dietary experts looking with disdain at anyone who raised a knife and a fork. Just the other day in the teachers' room, Rita Stanley, who just three months ago was sporting an overhang and a lardass, was pontificating on the evils of a regular Coke versus Diet Coke. A few months ago the bitch would down three regular Cokes at one sitting, washing down her honey-dipped donuts with them.

He decided to torment the witch. "I'll only have five or six before I pick you up," he finally replied.

"Oh, Chris! You're kidding! Please! For me? Be sober."

He chuckled into the phone. "Ma. Relax. I'll be sober. I don't drink Monday nights. It's my night off."

"Thank God for small favors," she said.

"Now, Ma. Today's not Monday. It's Friday. And I need to conclude my business meeting."

She couldn't resist. "Who ever heard of Friday evening business meetings at bars?" she said disdainfully.

"Ma, there's more business conducted at bars than anywhere else except maybe golf courses."

"I don't believe you."

"I got to go, Ma."

———

On Monday night Chris drove the short distance from his apartment on Bellevue Road up to the Union Hospital. Along the route he noted the usual army of cell phone users one-handing their vehicles out of the side streets, most of them looking only in the direction of the turn.

He parked his Taurus in the visitors' parking lot and entered the hospital at ground level, seeking out directions to the diabetes workshop meeting.

"Conference Room 101" read the makeshift sign posted to the wall just beyond the entrance.

When he opened the door to 101, he thought he had forgotten his own birthday. But May 12 wasn't his birthday.

Seated in a semicircle in the middle of a vast room were Norma, Marlene, Peter Gregory, his best friend Gil Barrett, his fellow teacher Harvey Blum, and his college mentor, Professor Driscoll from Salem State. And one other, a stranger who now rose to greet him.

"What the hell is this?" Chris blurted out, standing there in his Bermuda shorts, Polo shirt and K-Mart sneakers.

"Hello, Chris," said a tall and willowy six-footer, maybe thirty years old, with lightly gelled blond hair and watery blue eyes, a crucifix dangling from his left ear, narrow gold-rimmed glasses giving him, supposedly, the mark of a scholar. "I'm George Burton. Welcome." He extended a hand which Chris let dangle.

Chris sought out his mother. "Ma? This is a diabetes workshop?" he asked angrily.

"Allow me to explain," said Watery Eyes. "Your family and friends have gathered here this evening in support of you, Chris. Their attendance, their concern, their love are all indicative of their commitment."

George Burton then pointed to a seat at the top of the semicircle. "Please, Chris. Join us and help us make this intervention a positive experience."

Chris hesitated, trying to gather his thoughts, trying to control his anger at being mouse trapped. In that split second, Professor Driscoll stood and walked to him. "Chris, please. Have a seat. We're here only to be of help," said his old mentor now just a year away from retirement. Placing an arm around his shoulder, the elderly professor walked Chris to the seat, waited until he sat himself, and then patted Chris's hand before returning to his own position.

The little crucifix bounced around George Burton's ear, making him look a bit like Barry Bonds, as he smiled his appreciation at Professor Driscoll.

"Well, now, I think we can proceed. First of all, I want to thank you all for being here for Chris. Your willingness to assist him with his problem…"

"What problem?" Chris blurted out.

The interruption didn't slow down Watery Eyes. He had heard it all before. "Your drinking problem, Chris," he continued without missing a beat. "Through this intervention, through our sharing our feelings, our personal observations with you, we hope to assist you, to provide insight…"

What was he, a minister, Chris wondered as the bore droned on using big words, calling him by his first name, using pronouns like "we" and "our", the guy a complete stranger to him, Chris guessing the weirdo had plenty of problems of his own, like deciding which sex he was.

"So, as we discussed earlier, I would like each of you to share your feelings with Chris. Gil, would you begin for us?" Burton whimpered.

Staged. That's what it was. All prearranged, his family and few friends herded together to ream his ass, no matter what else they called it.

Sitting there, slouching, listening to Gil mouthing some babble about their past history, he wished he had taken a few belts before coming here. He felt like one of those nitwits on reality TV being judged by some celebrity, or like the guys being judged at Nuremberg. Maybe he should call a halt to the proceedings, or hire himself a lawyer like the guys who got O.J. Simpson off, someone to set him free.

"I've loved you for more than thirty years now, Chris," Gil was saying. Next he'll be planting a kiss on my cheek, like most men did today – pansy men.

"So I hate seeing you do this to yourself, man, y'know? We all come here tonight out of friendship – your family, your ex-wife, and your friends – to demonstrate our concern…"

Gil had always possessed the ability to string words together, Chris would give him that. Too bad he wasn't so explicit concerning his own problems.

"So you've become an embarrassment to us, to me, Chris, who loves you."

Sitting beside Chris, Watery Eyes nodded his encouragement. "Excellent, Gil. Let Chris know your true feelings. Tell it like it is."

Chris bit down on his lower lip to no avail. "Could I say something?" he asked, looking at Watery Eyes.

The master of ceremonies shook his head aggressively. "Chris, our intervention is best received through its cumulative effect. Please bear with us. Once you've heard comments from everyone, we would all welcome your response. Would we not, people?"

The group reminded him of a chorus of circus tigers, sitting there, nodding back at their trainer, hoping for another chunk of meat if they followed along dutifully.

"Are we ready to proceed?"

Fuck you, Chris thought.

"Peter." Watery Eyes nodded in recognition to Gregory. Calling him "Peter" created more of an edge in Chris. In all probability the two had never met until tonight. Peter, my ass.

"Chris knows of my feelings. I pride myself, as his principal, on my directness. I tell it like it is to our faculty and to our students. So my message, like me, is quick and decisive. Chris, you have to gain control of this problem. You need to enter an alcohol rehabilitation program over the summer months and get yourself straight. Now I'll be there in the fall at

Lynn English to offer support, that is if you're making progress, if you're sober. If you're regressing or still in this pattern of denial and absenteeism, then I'm going to do my job, union or no union."

Watery Eyes looked at Peter Gregory as if he had just received the Ten Commandments. "Excellent, Peter. Such honesty and directness are to be commended."

Chris crossed his arms in front of his chest and then quickly corrected himself before Burton or someone else could comment regarding his negative body language.

"Harvey?"

Harvey Blum, a short, full-bearded chemistry teacher, was usually a man of few words. Thank God for small favors, Chris felt, as Harvey spoke of his high regard for Chris, of his teaching prowess, of the potential loss of an outstanding teacher if Chris could not conquer his problem.

"We need good and dedicated teachers, Chris. You've been my friend and have given me advice concerning my teaching methodologies and now I am here tonight making myself available to you when you need me," he concluded.

Watery Eyes nodded once again in grateful acknowledgement. Somehow Chris had the idea that if one of the group suggested they attach electrodes to his vitals that would be just as eagerly received by Burton.

"Beautifully said. Now I would like Professor Driscoll to speak."

The other presenters had sat there, leaning slightly forward in their seats as they spoke, but Martin Driscoll needed to play a part. He stood slowly, calling attention to himself, gaining an inch, standing as if he intended to deliver a lecture which he undoubtedly would, Chris thought.

"Christopher, let us review some facts. And I ask you to consider the facts as we proceed." Chris stared at his science teacher. You would think he taught philosophy, standing there thinking of himself as Socrates, talking about facts, acting like a trial lawyer.

"When we first met, in your junior year I believe, I found a curious, dedicated young man eager to learn, eager to absorb knowledge, a young man fully focused on science, on the scientific method..."

God, Chris mused, could someone just pass him a drink, or better still give the old professor a drink, maybe a double?

"That promise has not been fulfilled Christopher. You know I detest heresay, but in recent years I have heard of your falling away from your calling. Yes, of your disinterest in the scientific method, in your profession. I have called you often over these years, have I not, Christopher? Called to ascertain why my calls, calls from your true mentor, have not been returned. Calls to see how I could be of assistance. To no avail, Christopher. In lieu of science, in lieu of friendship, you have turned to the bottle, to amber truth, rather than to scientific truth. Christopher..."

If the pompous ass mentioned science one more time, Chris was ready to pounce out of his chair and hammer him. Talk about Johnny One-note. All the pontifical bastard wanted to talk about was himself and how my actions impede on him, Chris thought.

"I want you to come about, Christopher, to come to an understanding that your falling away from the scientific life can be corrected. Place your faith in me, Christopher. Place your faith in science. I implore you to become the person I intended."

Watery Eyes touched his index finger to his lips. "Such a powerful presentation. Such feeling. You are to be commended, Professor, for presenting the truth so powerfully, so forcefully."

Chris clenched his fingers and then remembered to flex them, to not give any indication of his true feelings. Watery Eyes would be a connoisseur of body language, ready to jump on any early indication of tightness, of perceived resistance.

"And now we have our final two presenters," Watery Eyes was saying. "First, Chris's ex, Marlene."

Marlene leaned forward, smiling, the bitch not part of the problem, she was conveying. She placed her hands together intertwining them, giving an impression of placidity, of togetherness. A martyr.

"Chris, you and I were married for more than ten years," she began, adding a sigh to the words, letting the group know it had all been a burden. "I tried my best to make it work, to make a home for us, and I know you did, too, at least at the beginning. Do you remember the good times, Chris? I want to focus on those – our walks along Kings Beach, the dinner dates up in Essex. At Lewis's. Remember, Chris? The plays in Boston? You were so sweet over so many of those years. Such a gentleman." She paused for effect. Now here comes the shit, Chris mused.

"I don't know when or where it all began to unravel, Chris, but you stopped coming home evenings, stayed out drinking, and when you did come home you were loud, and Irish ugly, looking for a fight. I couldn't take it any more, and if you're listening to these people here – some of whom used to love you, all of whom still care – then you have to face up to your problem. Stop being the problem, and become part of the solution."

If he heard one more cliché, he vowed to vomit right there on the industrial rug.

Marlene signaled to Watery Eyes that she had finished.

"Mrs. Travis?"

The witch shook her head from side to side, a small tear working its way down the left side of her face. "I'm not going to say anything. Chris has heard plenty from me. He knows my feelings. He knows he's way out of control."

Watery Eyes nodded and played with his crucifix for a beat. "Well, Chris, you have heard now from everyone, all your "family" so to speak, all here to offer you assistance as you go forward."

"Fuck you and them, too."

Watery Eyes almost lost his composure. "I'm sorry? Excuse me, but did you say what I think you said?"

"Fuck you."

"Well, now, I never…"

Chris suddenly sat more erect, gaining a half-inch, ready to speak.

But the boss took control. "Now look, Chris…" Peter Gregory began, pointing an index finger.

"No, you look. You're about as quick and decisive as John Kerry, Peter. You ought to get quick and decisive with all the little shits smoking in the boys and girls rooms. Maybe get quick and decisive with those who can't teach instead of raggin' my ass. You're worried about my being absent a bit while minority kids are dropping out, while incompetents are posing as teachers. You got a problem with me, Peter, take it up with the unions. And you know what? They'll give a quick decisive answer to your quick and decisive self. In the meantime, fuck you."

The professor spoke before Watery eyes could shake his bewilderment. "Now, Chris, that is no way to treat your colleague. You must..."

"And you shut up too, you pompous ass..."

Watery Eyes tried to regain control of the meeting. "I must insist that we not enter into name calling, into projection, if you will."

The group stirred all at once, like an undulating wave ready to hit a beach wall. Eyes flittered left, and eyes flittered right, pleading for someone to gain control before they really did hit the wall.

Burton decided on another approach. "Christopher, you are in denial, and we can understand that. Perhaps by our presenting all these facts at one time..."

Time to hit Burton right between the eyes, cause a little more water to flow.

Chris pointed at him. "In the words of that famous social commentator, Homer Simpson, 'Facts are meaningless; you can use facts to prove anything that's even remotely true. Facts, schmacks.' "

Watery Eyes didn't know whether to believe his own ears. "I don't understand."

"That's right. You don't. None of you do."

"Are you saying we're all wrong, Chris?" Gil Barrett asked.

"You're worried about me, Gil? You who have gone through three wives already? Maybe if you kept your pecker in your pants you would still have the first wife."

Without hesitation, Gil lunged from his seat and launched himself at Chris. Balling his fists, he punched at Chris, causing him to fall back over the seat. On the way down Chris hit Marlene with the back of his hand. All the men rushed in to separate the combatants, Gil still trying to reach a prone Chris, who sought to right himself.

"Here! Here! We'll have none of this aggression!" screamed George Burton.

Chris stood, his arms pinned to his side by Gregory and Blum. "Get your hands off of me!" he screamed.

Burton looked like he was caught between a rock and a hard place. "Dear me! This will never do. If we don't all sit down at once, I'll have to call security."

Chris noted Marlene dabbling at her check with her Kleenex. "Are you all right?" he asked. "I didn't mean…"

She returned to her seat and sat. "I'm all right."

"Take your seats," Burton was directing, Chris half expecting him to add, "You naughties."

"Displacement. That's what we just observed here," Burton said, "Chris turning his problem on to someone else."

Chris looked at his hands and then to Watery Eyes. "Oh you mean Gil wasn't fucking around? He didn't attack me?"

Gil looked like he was ready for a second launching, but Marlene, sitting beside him, put a hand on his knee.

"Chris, we're only trying to help," she said soothingly.

"Oh really? Why did you leave me then, Marlene?"

Watery Eyes was not going to allow any more personal battles to go un-refereed.

"Now look here, Chris. Let's not personalize…"

Marlene raised her hand in the air. "Let me answer that please, George."

"Well, ordinarily…"

"Please."

"Go ahead."

"Why did I leave you, Chris? I think we've discussed the issue ninety-nine times. Because of your drinking naturally."

"My drinking," he repeated.

"Yes."

"Not your having an affair with the cop?"

"Chris! What are you talking about?" Marlene yelled.

Chris shook his head vigorously. "You got a nerve, Marlene. What came first? The chicken or the egg, the drinking or the cop?"

"I don't know what you're talking about," she huffed.

"Marriage and mating should be forever, Marlene. Like with pigeons and Catholics. I wanted that. You had to go and spoil it."

"I don't want to hear this!" Norma interrupted. "It's all your fault, you drunk! You've ruined this family with your drinking!" She stood, pointing an accusatory finger at him.

Directly across the circle from her, Chris stood also. "You should talk! Who introduced me to the stuff? Your face was always in the bottle…"

George Burton raced to the wall telephone. "This meeting has ended! I'm calling Security right now!"

"Be my guest!" Chris countered.

"I'm leaving," Peter Gregory announced. "This meeting is a disaster."

"And so aren't you!" Chris shouted.

Gregory quickly turned toward Chris and gave him the finger.

"Same to you!" Chris screamed.

"And forget about your teaching methodologies, Harvey," Chris said, pointing at his colleague. "Your problem isn't your methods. Your problem is you can't control your classes! When you can do that, then you can criticize me."

Harvey Blum hung his head sadly. "This just isn't right," he said.

At the door two security men dressed in blue uniforms entered warily. "Is there a problem here?" the older one asked.

"Yes, there is , officer," Chris replied. "This group is out of control."

JEALOUSY

From where Faye was standing the moist air smelled of salt water, and in the distance the orange towers of the Golden Gate stood shrouded in fog. If they were lucky, the fog might lift by 8:00 p.m., she thought, just in time for evening. But maybe not. Summer in Baghdad-by-the-Bay.

She stood at the rail opposite the doorway to their condo, debating with herself. Straight ahead she could just barely make out Alcatraz, like a sentinel guarding the Bay, its beacon flashing. Turning, she walked into a narrow living room furnished nicely with a brown leather sofa and two matching chairs. Opposite the fireplace, an extended wall contained two built-in bookcases loaded with the classics, as well as Jeff's law books. The room was immaculate.

She moved into the small kitchen to see if, by chance, the letter had disappeared, evaporated. But no, it was still there on one of the spotless marble countertops. Picking it up, she sat in one of the chairs next to the butcher block kitchen table and poured herself a shot of the Chivas, her eyes never once leaving the letter.

When the cell chirped she was startled back to reality. "Hi, sweetheart," Jeff said in his usual upbeat tone. "How's my one and only?"

His one and only? A weak smile creased Faye's lips. "Just fine, dear," she replied, trying to match his mood, but not wanting to.

"I'll be there in thirty minutes."

"Where are you?"

"On California Street. What's for dinner?"

"I'm cooking some lasagna."

"I can smell the oregano and the Parmesan."

"No, you can't," she snickered.

"Love you," he said.

But did he? Really?

She pictured him in his Armani suit, the golden hair slicked back, covered by sunglasses. Her gorgeous hunk. Her muscle-bound stud. Her budding superstar husband, San Francisco's most up and coming civil litigator.

"Hurry, darling," she finally replied.

Then she made the decision. After all, one could only consider alternatives so long. Either she trusted him or she didn't. Either she believed in their love, or she was suspicious enough to question it.

Standing, she studied the envelope one more time. The 4 X 7 white envelope was addressed to "Mr. Jeff Ferris, 602 Geary Street, San Francisco" from "Winters, 102 K Street, Washington, D.C." in an irregular but distinctively feminine scroll.

It was the Washington D.C. address that piqued her interest. That and the fact that it seemed every other woman in San Francisco had eyes for her husband. How many times had she observed women fawning about him at cocktail parties, touching him, trying to attract him with their bedroom eyes and extended stares? And how many times had friends warned her, kiddingly they claimed, that Jeff could have them anytime, anyplace.

Faye forgot the letter for a moment and sought out the mirror in the living room. Her profile stared back at her. She was waif-thin, and her five foot, four inch frame was frail. Whatever she did to her long, dark hair somehow always gave way to a tangle. Some said she was pretty, but she knew most regarded her as plain.

She assured herself she wasn't paranoid, but no one could be nastier than so-called friends, especially after a drink or two. "How do you ever corral him, Faye? You lucky girl, you!" they would say.

She studied the letter once again. Didn't she trust her own husband? Had she ever found cause for this feeling? Had she ever seen him appear interested in any of the twits throwing themselves at him? No to all questions. But she still wondered.

Besides, the letter had come from Washington. Just four years ago Jeff, a Bostonian, had finished Georgetown Law, but whenever she inquired about that period in his life, he had little to say.

When he moved to The City in 2000, he first worked as a public defender for the court over on Seventh and Bryant at the Hall of Justice. They had met by chance in a restaurant in Chinatown, she not believing initially that such a man would be interested in her. But one thing led to another, and eventually to bed, and to a proposal. Soon after, she had convinced him, seemingly too easily, that his future lay with her father and the law firm of Pendergast, Pendergast, and Wiley.

She glanced at her watch. Still plenty of time to open the letter. After all, she was his wife. But he had always insisted on some measure of privacy in their relationship – what was his, including mail, was his and what was hers was hers.

Faye chewed on her lower lip for a second and then moved to the stove, letter in hand, holding it over the steaming lasagna until the flap loosened appreciably. Moving quickly, she sat at the table and cast a concerned look toward the door. No question, she would hear him coming. The elevator made enough racket to warn a deaf man. Utilizing the letter opener, she carefully undid the flap, being sure not to cause a tear. Perfect.

She heaved a long sigh and began reading the poorly formed, disjointed script:

"Dearest Jeff, How long has it been since we last met? Six months by my calculation. Too long. Six months since I last felt your warm touch and your tender kiss.

I've missed you so much since your last visit to Washington. Do you remember our walk to the Washington Monument, running up the hill together holding hands? Like little kids.

I love you, Jeff. I always have and I always will. Ever since we first met when you were in college.

Could you visit Washington again anytime soon? If not, I think I could join you anywhere if you give me sufficient notice.

How is work going for my golden boy? Do you like San Francisco any better?

It's humid in Washington this time of year. Remember sitting on the steps of the Lincoln Memorial eating an ice cream when that guy insulted me out of the blue, and you tore into him? My hero.

Come see me soon.

Love, Danielle"

Faye might have stared at the letter for close to five minutes, trying to re-read passages against the rush of emotional waves riding over her, trying to capture nuances when words were blurring, the full impact overwhelming her, making it all the more difficult to absorb.

Around her the unremitting silence proved deafening. She tried to stand but barely stabilized herself by leaning into the table.

Danielle? She had never met or heard of any Danielle. Stop, she cautioned herself. Start at the beginning. Piece things together logically.

Nothing made sense, but everything was perfectly clear. This Danielle went all the way back to his time at Georgetown, a college sweetheart who her husband recently fought over! Think, she told herself. Six months ago would have been late December. Yes. Jeff had been away, supposedly representing the firm, just prior to Christmas.

And what about the part concerning leaving San Francisco? What had the whore written? Faye scanned the letter to find the appropriate place. "Do you like San Francisco any better?" What the hell did that mean? She had never heard he did not enjoy the city. Was he serious about relocating? Leaving her for a floozy?

A huge frown crossed Faye's face. Was he considering leaving both her and the firm? Jeff had never expressed any such thought, nor had he ever complained about working for her father.

She caught herself. Well, not directly he hadn't, but always right there beneath the surface she thought she read some resistance to her father who could be pushy and a bit arrogant. Just as she suspected Jeff's dishonesty regarding other women, it now appeared he had been dishonest about his personal happiness, obviously complaining to a whore with whom he had been conducting an affair for years.

She was startled by the sound of the elevator engaging. She slid the letter back into the envelope, ran her tongue over the flap, and sealed it. Walking into the living room, Faye deposited it with the rest of the correspondence.

She heard his call as the lock turned. "Darling, I'm home."

Stay cool, she warned herself. Show no sign of her concern. Bargain for time to think.

"Thanks for the warning," she responded gaily as Jeff headed straight for the bar across the room.

"Can I get something for you?" he asked sweetly.

"Yes. Chivas, please. How was your day?" she asked.

He wiggled a hand in the air. "So so. You know that Knowles case we've been working on – your dad and me?"

"The one about the development project out in Marin?"

"Right. Well, it's keeping us busy – 24/7."

She stood near the stool as he handed her the drink from across the bar. "Here you go," he said. "How's the lasagna coming along?"

"It needs three or four minutes. Why don't you relax while I see to it," she replied, thinking on the letter, not the pasta.

"Any mail?"

"On the table," she answered from over her shoulder as she walked to the kitchen.

She set the Caesar salad on the table and placed small portions of the lasagna on the huge plates. She heard the sounds of mail opening, waited a few minutes, and then called the question.

"Anything interesting?" she asked.

"Just the usual ads," he replied, almost too quickly.

"I thought I saw a letter from Washington, D.C.," she yelled.

"Just an ad," he replied dismissively.

—

By breakfast she welcomed the respite from a sleepless, difficult night. He had lain there serene, sound asleep, completely unaware of the turmoil rushing like a train at her.

Should she confront the liar directly, or wait for even more proof? Over ham and eggs the question was answered for her.

"I didn't mention it last night, but something has come up that will necessitate my taking a trip," he announced out of the blue.

"Really? I thought the Knowles case had your total attention?"

He spread some margarine over his toast. "There's a legal convention next week that offers some topics that will help your dad and me with the Knowles matter."

She didn't have to ask where the convention would be held, but she did anyway.

"Where will you be going?"

"Washington," he replied unhesitatingly. "But I first need to clear it with your dad."

—

When she was alone, she had almost too much time to think with Chivas as her only counsel. And she didn't need that, not at 9:00 a.m. Instead, she sat facing the Pacific watching the ant-like cars across the bridge, sipping her coffee, considering things.

She could call her father and tell him not to allow the trip, couldn't she? No, she couldn't. If her father confronted Jeff, that would be the end of their relationship. And there was no way her father wouldn't get involved once he knew of his baby's concern.

Or she could approach Jeff directly, seek an explanation, demand to know what was going on. Yes, she could and she would once he was home.

She caught herself. Having too much time alone to think was as bad as too little. She loved him, didn't she? If she accused him directly, he would lie in all probability. What good would it do?

Faye bit into her lower lip, drawing a faint line of blood. How many times had she pictured him in some other woman's arms? How many times had her jealousy been aroused by some other woman's touch? How many Danielles were really out there?

Danielle wasn't the problem, Jeff was. Her philandering husband was. She loved him, didn't she? No, she didn't. Not if she couldn't trust him. If he wasn't all hers, then she didn't want him at all. But that wasn't quite true. She would see him dead rather than with another woman.

—

The plan was easy enough to execute. God bless creatures of habit, she thought. On Wednesday, the evening before his trip, Jeff planned to eat an early dinner and retire early. Always unable to sleep well the night before an early morning flight, Jeff enjoyed the filet mignon and then took his sleeping pill. To be sure he slept well, Faye added a second pill to his martini.

Sleep well, my love. For all eternity, she thought as he bent to kiss her in the middle of one of O'Reilly's diatribes against same sex marriage.

"I'm going to bed now," Jeff whispered in her ear. "I love you," he said, running his fingers through her hair.

"And I you," she responded to the cheater. "Forever," she added. How would he know forever wouldn't last very much longer.

—

She stayed awake watching an old movie, the film not registering at all, her thoughts completely on the task at hand. After an hour she tiptoed gracefully toward the open bedroom door and stood there silently, listening for Jeff's breathing rhythms or for any sign indicating he was sleeping restlessly.

Her dad was such a prince she thought as she headed back to the kitchen. "Of course you can come over. We'll be up," he had said, knowing she hated being alone at such an early evening hour.

Before she left the flat, she ensured all windows were closed and turned on the gas.

—

"Such a tragedy," Faye's good friend Dolly Hayes was saying, pressing her lily white handkerchief to her face. "So young and such a virile, handsome man. Only thirty-two years old."

Faye stood beside the bier in her plain black dress, remembering to keep her own handkerchief close, alternatingly dabbing at her eyes or wrapping it about her fingers, playing the role of the grieving widow. "Thanks for being here for me Dolly," she whispered.

To her right her father stood long and tall, Paul Pendergast surveying the crowd like an emperor of his flock. The line weaved its way back out to Geary Street as most of San Francisco's elite came to pay respect.

"I should have been there for him, Dolly," Faye whimpered, pressing the hanky to her eyes.

Her father drew her into his embrace. "Don't torture yourself, my darling. The police feel he must have gotten up after you left. He probably went to make some coffee and left the stove on by accident."

"Don't blame yourself, Faye," Dolly said.

"She's right you know. The police found a half-filled cup of coffee in the bedroom. It all makes sense. The pills and all."

As each mourner kneeled to pray in front of the open casket, Faye noticed that all the young women were crying, not the older ones. Which ones had he bedded she wondered. The leggy blonde in the velvet hat? The diminutive redhead in the short skirt? The brunette with the big boobs? Probably all of them.

It was just then that she observed the odd couple. About five yards from the kneeler, an elderly priest held the arm of a young girl, perhaps twelve, dressed in a white blouse and a blue pleated skirt. What was odd was that the priest was guiding the girl.

As they reached the coffin, the priest directed the young girl to genuflect with him. They knelt together in silent prayer, made the Sign of the Cross in tandem, and stood.

"Mrs. Ferris, I am terribly sorry," the priest said. "May I offer you my condolences?"

"Thank you, Father."

"I am Father Arthur Doyle from St. Francis School in Washington, D.C."

At the mention of Washington, Faye became instantly alert. "And this is Danielle Winters, one of my constituents," he added.

The blind girl extended her hand, "I'm sorry," she said sweetly.

"Danielle? From Washington?" Faye heard herself asking as she sought composure, as pressure mounted in her chest.

"Yes," the girl replied.

"We're dear friends of Jeff's," the priest said.

The young girl began to sob.

Placing an arm about her, Father Doyle drew her close. "Danielle is physically challenged, but, as you can see, she is a beautiful person, a loving person who thought so much of Jeff."

"A friend?" Faye said, not really knowing what to say. "A student?"

"We knew Jeff from Georgetown," the priest said. "He told you of his sister?"

Faye knew that much. "Laura? Yes, she died of cancer in her teens," Faye said.

"And she was blind," Father Doyle said.

"Yes. But…"

"Jeff was at Georgetown at the time. When his sister passed away in Boston, he began to support our school, to help others who are blind."

"I don't understand, Father. He never told me of any financial…"

The priest raised a hand. "No, no, my dear. He gave his heart – to Danielle and to our other students. Whenever he could, he came back to Washington to give us the most precious gift of all – his time. He was our benefactor, our friend."

Faye placed a shaky hand to her forehead. Observing her, Father Doyle reached for it. "I am so sorry, my dear. He was our friend, and I his priest. Let me tell you, I have never met a man so pure of heart."

ABOUT THE AUTHOR

John A. Curry is President Emeritus of Northeastern University. He is a graduate of that university and earned his doctorate from Boston University. From 1989-1996, he served as President of Northeastern University, changing its direction from a large, urban institution toward a more selective "smaller but better" university.

He has written four novels – <u>Loyalty</u>, <u>Two and Out</u>, <u>The Irish Corsicans</u>, and <u>Bless Me Father</u>, as well as one other collection of short stories, <u>Some Shorts in the Dark</u>, all available through Author House, 1663 Liberty Drive, Bloomington, Indiana 47403.

Dr. Curry lives in Saugus, Massachusetts, where he is currently working on a new novel.

Printed in the United States
24480LVS00002B/40-315